SOLDIER OF THE EMPIRE

Red Dawn I

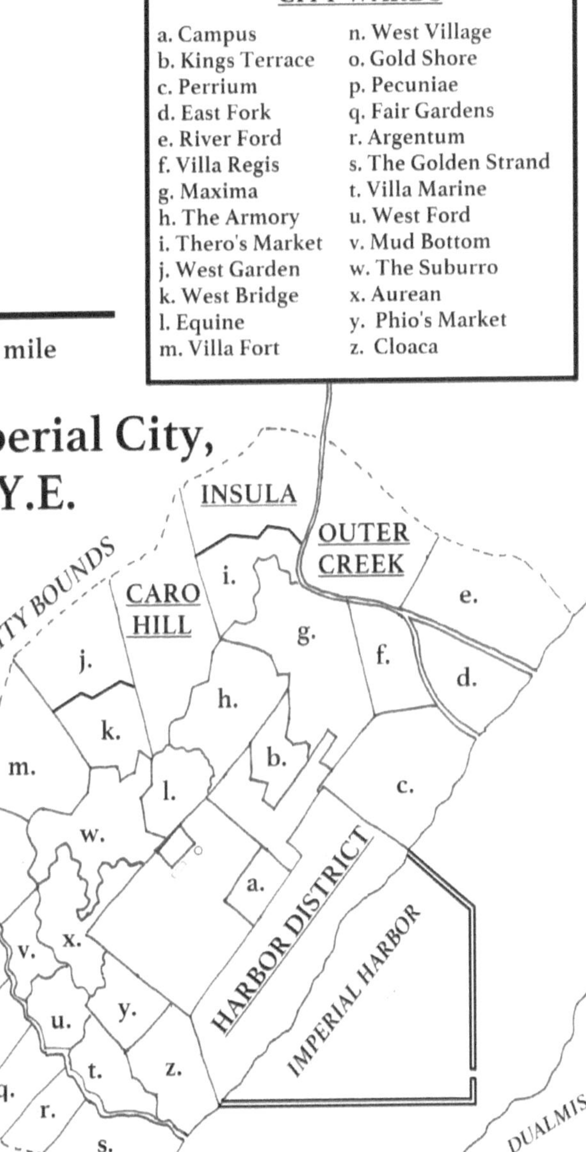

CITY WARDS

a. Campus
b. Kings Terrace
c. Perrium
d. East Fork
e. River Ford
f. Villa Regis
g. Maxima
h. The Armory
i. Thero's Market
j. West Garden
k. West Bridge
l. Equine
m. Villa Fort
n. West Village
o. Gold Shore
p. Pecuniae
q. Fair Gardens
r. Argentum
s. The Golden Strand
t. Villa Marine
u. West Ford
v. Mud Bottom
w. The Suburro
x. Aurean
y. Phio's Market
z. Cloaca

1 mile

Imperial City, 210 Y.E.

INSULA
OUTER CREEK
CITY BOUNDS
CARO HILL
HARBOR DISTRICT
IMPERIAL HARBOR
DUALMIS

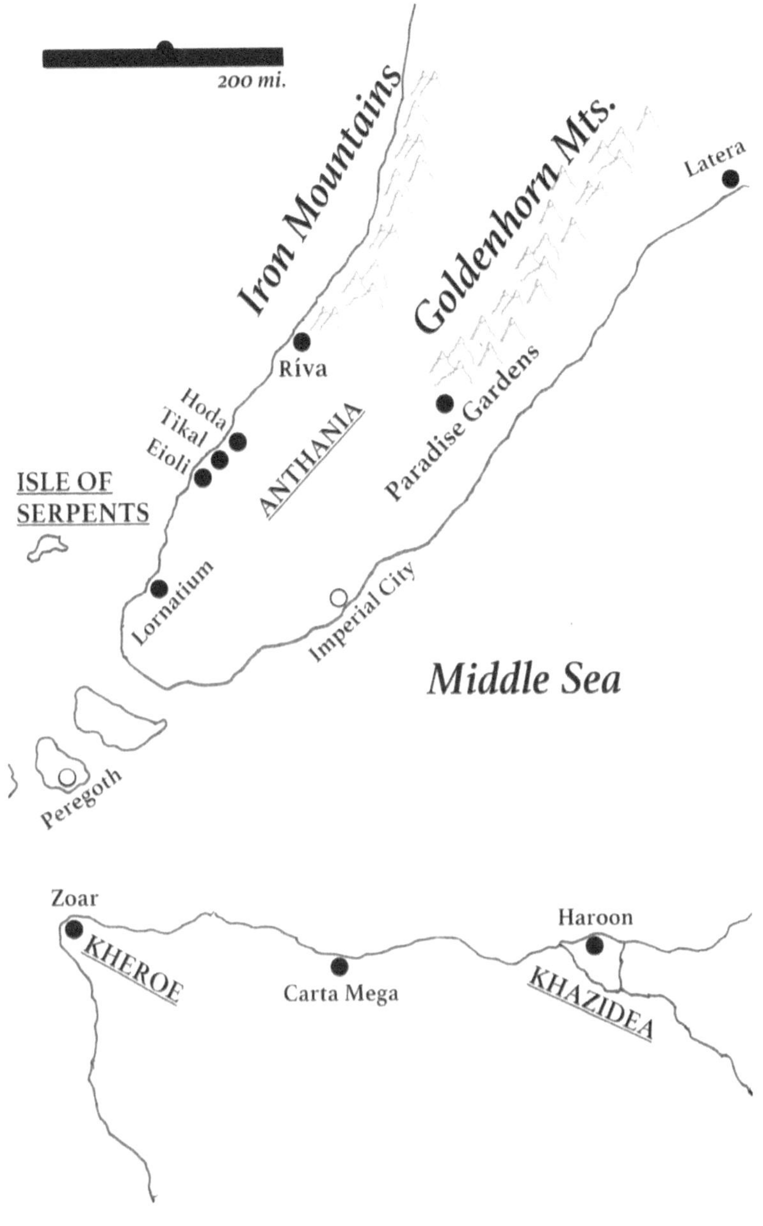

200 mi.
Iron Mountains
Goldenhorn Mts.
Latera
Ríva
Hoda
Tikal
Eioli
ANTHANIA
Paradise Gardens
ISLE OF
SERPENTS
Lornatium
Imperial City
Middle Sea
Peregoth
Zoar
Haroon
KHEROE
Carta Mega
KHAZIDEA

Red Skies

The skies were red over Imperial City.

Red they were, and orange, and yellow, as if they had caught flame.

In the harbor of the city, frightened sailors hurried to shore. In temples, priests consulted the gods, and in the streets the people talked in hushed tones, wondering if the end had come.

Amid the panic of the moment, rumors began to circulate, and under the fiery sky dark words began to spread, that the emperor's daughter had been kidnapped the previous night, that assassins had taken her. And in the north, there was news that the barbarians were on the march.

Yes, it was the end of the world, the people of Imperial City thought. But in the morning the skies cleared, and the waters of the harbor were still and blue.

Part One

Chapter One

Publius Allius Corvus

Publius had never wanted to be a soldier.

As he sprinted through the fields with his fellow recruits, he pondered that thought, and held it close to his heart.

But there had never been another option for him, not in any real sense. His father, a tailor in the flea-bitten slums of Imperial City, had passed on the family business to his brother, and so, when Publius reached the age of manhood and donned his tunic for the first time, he had heeded the call of his country; he had heeded the call that so many had, some to the ultimate cost.

The sprint eased.

They were somewhere several hundred miles north of Imperial City, well outside its bounds. Somewhere nearby were the lush villas and parks of Paradise Gardens, where the wealthy members of the Imperial Council would retreat in the summer. It was now spring, and despite a gentle breeze blowing, Publius was drenched in sweat. Over the past few weeks, the morning jogs, up and down hills, and sometimes through the mountains, had become easier and easier. Publius had built up endurance, endurance his tribune insisted would be needed on long marches.

The recruits, three hundred in number, completed their circle through a stand of pines and cypresses, and slowed their jog to a walk. The tents and open air plazas of base camp came into focus, and so too did the form of a centurion in full regalia. His black-plated armor was brightened by a red-and-gold tabard, and the crest of his helmet was brilliant, the color of blood.

Publius wondered what a full soldier was doing here, in official garb nonetheless. The recruits of Blue Eagle Camp were young; and their initiation into the legions was some year away.

The green recruits ended their run at the dirt square in the center of camp. The centurion was standing there, eyeing the recruits, examining them like a farmer would his cattle. His eyes were the most piercing blue Publius had ever seen, the color of the sky, the color of the ocean. They were cold as well, unfeeling, as they went from recruit to recruit. He and Publius exchanged glances, and Publius immediately looked away.

"Men of Blue Eagle Camp." The centurion's voice was crisp and clear, and he had an aristocratic accent. "I have good news on behalf of the emperor, on behalf of Imperium. We are taking a small number of you and moving you up to the rank of full legionary; we are advancing you beyond your training, and accepting you immediately into the Second Anthanian Legion."

Publius, panting, was too tired to think much of his words, too exhausted from the morning run. It made little sense. They were green and inexperienced; and now they were to join the Empire's forces?

"I have this on the authority of the emperor," the centurion said. "I bear with me the command of Imperium; I have laid on the bedrolls of the chosen a tabard. If you find you have been chosen, meet me at Blue Gate at once."

~

When Publius went to his tent, he saw indeed a tabard there, a black tabard with a gold moon in the center of it. Some of his exhaustion had cleared away, and confusion abounded then.

Lucius, one of his tent mates, slapped him on the back. "You are one of the lucky ones," he said.

But Publius did not feel lucky. Quite the opposite. He could barely wield his sword with his shield in tow; he did not know the least bit of strategy. He would be incompetent on the field of battle, a liability to his men and to the legion itself. It was as astounding as it was preposterous.

But nonetheless, Publius picked up his tabard, folding it and pressing it to his breast. He had sworn an oath of loyalty to the Empire, to his tribune, to the Imperial Army and to the nation itself. He wandered out of the tent into the cool morning air.

~

Thirteen recruits were there in total, Publius included, who had been given black and gold tabards.

The centurion's piercing blue eyes were like sapphires in the sun's light. "All of you. You have been chosen. I bring you congratulations at the behest of the emperor. He has personally selected each of you. And now we leave. To the mountains we go."

The mountains. Was that where the Second Anthanian Legion was posted? There were wars far off, in the north, and far south across the sea. But the mountains were a strange place for the Second Anthanian. The Goldenhorns were mostly bereft of people, and though the Empire had good reason to protect its iron and silver mines, what threat was there to protect them from?

Unease had settled into Publius, yes, unease, and his stomach was twisting to knots. His sword was buckled to his side, his shield to his back, and in the journey ahead, however long it took them, he prayed he would not have use for them.

Chapter Two

Publius Allius Corvus

They departed in the night, after sundown.

Crickets were chirping and in the dark, the outlines of mountains and hills were like black shadows. Cypresses wafted in the breeze, and in the dry cold air Publius found himself able to move, able to breathe, more easily than in the heat of the day. On rocky outcrops grew fruits-of-paradise, their red bulbous berries nestled among green leaves, inviting to the eye but poisonous to the taste. Such was life in the foothills, a place where things never were as they seemed.

Some time very late, when the moon was out, bright white, a waning crescent, and when the stars were advanced in their nightly procession, the centurion who called himself Caro halted his walk and gave the orders… they were to prepare for bed.

"We resume at dawn," Caro said.

Publius undid his bedroll from his pack and laid it on the grass. In the darkness, his fear had grown, his unsurety of what was going on. They were headed to the mountains… why? There were wars in the north and in the south, but the mountains… something didn't sit right with him.

But the weariness of the day and the long night began to catch up with him. He had lain down only a minute before he had shut his eyes and fallen asleep.

He dreamed that night of a little temple in a little forest, and in that little temple was dark shadow, and in that shadow, a human figure.

Chapter Three

Tidus Sulpicius Varro, Marshal of the Guard

Varro, Marshal of the Guard, had witnessed many things in his career: assassinations, poisonings, conspiracies against and within the Imperial family.

But as he walked the Imperial Palace's white marble corridors, he realized he had never encountered anything quite like this.

He was returning, as he had every day for the past few weeks, to the scene of the crime.

At the threshold of Julia's door, he stopped once again. It was open, now, and on the night that Julia vanished it had been slightly ajar, when she had always kept it locked.

Varro walked in, feeling the breeze from the open window. The window took up much of the wall, and its yellow curtains fluttered in the wind. One could see the entirety of the city below, and far away the gleaming celestial blue of the sea. One could see the Imperial hippodrome, even watch and bet on the games from so great a height.

It was a reminder of the opulence of the Imperial family, no less than the gold-dyed silk curtains, the banisters and the benches, the tables of teak and the white urns and the cotton sheets. The entirety of Julia's floor was a mosaic, displaying some ancient battle, the Eloesians against the southrons. There were silver jugs on the dining table, paintings bordered in gold, nude statues, and display cases filled with jewelry. Julia was a pampered, spoiled princess, the kind the ancient Imperials, the old stock, would have loathed and driven out of their cities. The Imperials had fought a war against kings; and now they had one of their own.

In his time as Marshal of the Guard, Varro had not seen

Julia much, but he had heard of her demanding ways, and he'd witnessed her shouting at the palace servants. She had been born into the purple, the daughter of Marcus Seánus, a member of the most blueblooded family in the Empire. She was devoutly religious, too, to all the gods. But she was gone.

It was a week ago, the eve of the Rite of Spring, when it happened. In the morning, the servants had come by with her specially prepared food to find her bed empty, urns shattered, and the great window open. The wall had been smeared with blood, indicating injury, and instantly Varro—and the emperor—believed the worst.

A breeze was blowing in from the open window, ruffling the silk curtains. Varro looked around, not sure what he was searching for, just hoping—perhaps in vain—that something would catch his eye, that he would find some clue that would unlock the mystery of what had occurred.

The blood was still there; it had not been cleaned up. Everything was as it had been that night, and nothing had been taken away; all was in its place, and only Varro and the most senior of the Imperial Guard were allowed in. It was they, and the urban cohorts they commanded, that were in charge of the rescue operation, but in the week since Julia disappeared, nothing had been uncovered.

Still he looked, and he searched, and he began to walk across the mosaic floors. The silver jar of water was overturned near the window; the bits of glass reflected in the sunlight, at least, those bits of glass that hadn't been stuck to Varro's boots. He walked to the edge of the window.

The Imperial Palace was an immense complex, a city more than it was a house. Below, many fathoms, was the grass of a hill, blooming with purple wildflowers. The hill itself descended into the streets below. He wondered... he pondered... He questioned whether Julia had been taken down there, if somehow, she managed to climb down, though Varro couldn't imagine a ladder so tall, so, so many fathoms high. If Varro jumped it would kill him instantly. Yet Julia had been seen before sitting on the window's edge, singing or praying, in the middle of the night.

It was worth a try, even if it amounted to nothing.

~

Varro spent the next hour trying to find his way to that grassy hill beneath Julia's window. It became more and more clear that there was no easy way to get there. The entirety of the Imperial Palace was like a maze, a maze with thick brick walls, and the only doors that led outside seemed to lead to the garden.

But the garden, a place of blooming lilacs, fig trees and basil, was not where Varro wanted to go.

Varro twisted his way through the kitchen, seeing scullions hard at work preparing the noon meal, their faces and hands covered in flour, and on a table a great torte cake decorated in icing. He found the passageway he'd seen before, a dark shadowy tunnel. He ventured through it, and again found himself in the garden, the damned garden.

In the garden overgrown with lilacs and flowers, there were fresh fruits and vegetables, some ripe for the plucking, and innumerable fig trees which the emperor loved. The morning was bright and warm, and the sun was shining on the greenery.

He recalled the palace window, where the emperor's daughter sat, faced the hippodrome and Imperial Square. Perhaps, if he retraced his steps, he could head out into the rough-and-tumble world of Imperial City, and make his way back to that patchy hill.

~

Varro, as Marshal of the Guard, did not like to spend his time in Imperial City. It was dangerous, yes, as all cities were, but it reminded him of how far it had fallen. Once it had been a military camp, a place that despised luxury and softness, and seeing the rabbit's warren of taverns and brothels sickened him. At the gate of the Imperial Palace he departed, glaring at a piper playing a sultry tune. Merchants had set up shop outside the great plaza, and apartment buildings crowded out the sky. Refuse was everywhere, and in the sunlight the stink was wafting upwards, forming a putrid miasma.

Just across the street from the Imperial Palace, the heart of the nation, the apartments were slumping, the tiles of the roof hanging roughshod, the iron of the water pumps lined with rust. There were homeless people, bedraggled, garbed in rags, proffering bowls to anyone who would deign to feed them. And running through the street was a band of recruits, conscripted for the legion, reminding Varro of this cesspool's origins… a military camp, a place of respect and of honor.

Varro turned down the road, and though he would stick out among the unwashed masses, he was girt in a breastplate, with a sword at his side, and he could more than take care of himself.

~

At the hippodrome, the noise of a game was echoing. The sun beat hot on the white pavestones of the streets. Varro wanted to remove his helmet, but he knew he could not.

The Imperial Palace was mounted on its hill, a white rider on a green horse, a gleaming marble complex that stretched to the sky, full of towering piazzas and turrets that scraped against the blue. To its left was the spiraling Council House which was connected by a sky bridge.

So many windows of the palace looked down on the streets

below it was impossible for Varro to know where to begin. But he would begin, yes, he would begin. He had come this far. He would finish what he started.

Varro pressed beyond the crowds, the merchants hawking their wares, the prostitutes offering their services underneath the sun, and began to ascend up the ground. Dilapidated buildings clung to the grassy hill, and then, there it was, a great black iron fence, keeping the common citizens away from the palace.

The air was sweltering as Varro made his way along the black fence, past overgrown gardens and abandoned homes. Through the cloying bushes he ventured, walking beside the fence, following a hunch, a feeling, a thought that was not fully formed, one he could not put to words.

The grass was bent in places, as if it had been walked through; the leaves of the bushes were torn off twigs. In the shadow of an abandoned apartment building, he stopped; a three-foot length of iron fence had been sawed off, enough for a person to squeeze through. And hidden among tufts of grass, a length of metal gleamed.

It was a pendant with its golden chain broken, as if had been torn off someone's neck. He recognized it instantly as the symbol of the Seáni family.

The "princess" had been here, the emperor's daughter. The thieves, the kidnappers… whoever had taken her… they had taken her through this broken bit of fence. And then, well, then, what had they done with her?

Varro stooped down and grabbed the pendant. He opened pendant to find a gleaming white diamond in the center.

"Where are you?" he said. "Where are you, Julia? Tell me."

~

When Varro returned to the Imperial Palace, he told no one

about what he found. He hid the broken pendant in his cloak until he returned to his room. Then, not knowing exactly why, he swore to tell no one, at least, until he found out what happened for himself.

Chapter Four

Achiba

For days, the Empire had encamped around the city of Eioli, and for days Achiba had kept quiet as his mother asked, and stayed holed up in his room.

Occasionally he would hear great stones rain down, hurled from catapults by the vicious Imperials. But in the past hour—it was evening—things seemed to have quieted.

Achiba's father Haddan was somewhere out there, fighting, and when Achiba thought about that, he had to close his eyes, and try to distract himself. He had asked his mother why the Empire wanted to kill them, and his mother said it was for gold.

At one time, not long ago, the land of Ugarit had been free, doing as they would and living as they wanted.

He had learned of the Empire's first war against the Ugars, how every city, every single city, had agreed to become subservient allies—every city except one, Eioli. Once, there had been many cities like Eioli, many places where people like Achiba staked out their lives in prosperity and peace. The Ugars warred amongst themselves, yes, but a foreign threat had arrived from foreign shores, and in the twinkling of an eye the world had changed. A new foe was on the march, and those Ugars who would not submit to the Empire were faced with death, or far worse.

A loud crack echoed, like thunder, followed by the crashing of a collapsing building. One of the catapults had struck home. Screams rung out, desperate wails, lighting up the night as more boulders fell like thunder. The Imperials were ruthless; for more than a century after Anthans' troops landed, the Ugars had been left in peace… but then, for reasons Achiba did not understand, the Imperials turned on them in cruelty, focusing all their hatred on

Eioli… on the city of Eioli, where Achiba lived, where gold there was, where the Ugars still breathed free.

The night was deep, and through Achiba's window he could see the moon was rising, veiled in a white cloud. The stars were out, even the Bull constellation, which represented Eioli's chief god Belpheor. Perhaps, it was a sign from Belpheor, a sign that things were about to change, that the Imperials were about to be driven away, that the cities of the coast would rise up and join their sister Eioli.

"Achiba!" his mother called from the other room, beside herself, and Achiba ran into the main hall.

"We take shelter!" she said.

Achiba's sister Borah and his little brother Lamman were there with Mother, clutching her tight.

Achiba knew where they were going: to Eioli's donjon-keep. That could only mean bad things for the defenders on the wall, for Achiba's father. It was Father out there fighting, Father and the city's able bodied men, battling in desperation, so that the name of the Ugars would never pass from memory, so that the cities of the coast would remain standing forever.

Lamman wailed as Mother jerked them toward the door. Out into the brisk night air the family fled, Achiba tagging along behind them.

It was almost like the brightness of the day, so many fires were burning. The house across the street had been completely smashed to rubble, and the dark form of a boulder flickered massively in the unsteady light.

The moon was radiant, the stars pinpricks of light amid the rising smoke. The smell of death was in the air, death and burnt flesh. In the distance, panicked screams rang out, a family hobbling through the wreckage, warriors running this way and that, and a brigade of men dousing the fires with water. Panic had consumed the city of Eioli, a city that had once been the richest in the world, a city that had gleamed and prospered when Imperial City was a collection of tents. That was Eioli, yes, that was Eioli, Achiba's home.

And look what had become of her… look at the scattered wreckage. Achiba stopped to mourn for her, for the glory that was lost, for the glory that might never return, all because the Imperials were greedy, all because the Imperials wanted their gold.

"Come on!" Mother screamed, and Achiba was jerked from his thoughts. He took off at a run through the dark, dim lit streets, illuminated only by distant fires. He choked on the smoke as he made his way toward the donjon-keep. He thought of his father.

Eioli was falling; it was falling, and there was nothing Achiba could do.

Chapter Five

Tidus Sulpicius Varro, Marshal of the Guard

Three days had passed since Varro found the pendant, three days and three nights since he placed it in his room, and as the morning light filtered through his window, a lone ray touched the gold, and the white star within. The chain was broken, as if it had been ripped from Julia's neck, and it convinced Varro more than anything that she had not left of her own free will, that she had been taken.

Julia, or Julia Ultima as some mockingly called her, was a princess in a nation that loathed royalty. She had been spoiled from her earliest days, born on the Isle of Peregoth in a mansion called Starhome, and spent her summers in a villa in Paradise Gardens. She was cross sometimes, and high minded, full of sour energy, but the palace slaves were devoted to her and were truly aggrieved at her disappearance. She seemed to have won their loyalty, something her father Marcus Seánus had never done.

The white star radiated whenever sunlight touched it; it was like a true star, plucked from the night sky. Varro had placed it on his balcony, and when he saw that pendant he thought of Julia, and rededicated himself to finding her.

He had told no one, for he trusted no one in the Imperial Palace, nor did he trust the members of the guard. Politics drew the worst of men, and from all the Empire's lands the worst of the worst came, filling the offices and rooms. Any one of them could be in on the plot, any one of them whom Varro trusted. A cesspool of ambition the Imperial Palace was, and not even the emperor was safe.

Julia Ultima had been in her bedroom that night; she had been taken, somehow, from that window, and been forcibly removed. The fence keeping out the refuse of Imperial City had been broken. But why had Julia been taken? For what reason was she gone? And who would want to abduct her?

Varro cinched his belt, draped his red half-cape over his shoulder, and exited his room. The sun had arisen, and now it was his duty to guard the emperor.

The emperor was on the Great Porch, which overlooked the hippodrome and Imperial Square. He was garbed in purple, with a gold necklace around his neck. His fingers were studded with rings and jewelry; his nose was aquiline, his face handsome and young-looking for the forty years he had been on this earth.

"Any news?" the emperor said.

Varro shook his head. "I continue to search for her," he said. "We are questioning some people in the city. I promise I will find you answers, Your Excellency."

The emperor nodded. "I have a speech today," he said as servants buttoned his tunic and adjusted his belt. "Care to hear it before I deliver it?"

"Of course, Your Excellency," Varro said. "I am at your service always."

The emperor cleared his throat.

He extended his hand, and his eyes seemed to twinkle, as if he were truly giving the speech in the Council House. "Men of the Imperial Council... distinguished citizens all... I bring you news good and bad from the far corners."

Varro had learned to suppress his laughter, to feign interest and deference. It was a skill he'd acquired in the nest of vipers called the Imperial Palace.

"The campaign in the barbarian coastlands is approaching its end. The Fourth Peregothian Legion lies encamped around the last rebel city, Eioli, and Legate Lentulus has been entrusted with seeing the mission to its conclusion. But as we increase our grip in the cities of Ugarit let us remember our calling, that the Empire seeks no conquests or dominations, but only to support our allies."

"You are a good liar," Varro said, and in an instant, the emperor snapped out of his delusion. He was no longer in the council chamber, no longer staring at the thirty old men in white tunics and purple sashes.

"All I said was true," the emperor insisted.

Did he truly believe? Marcus Seánus really thought it was true, that the Empire's military adventures were selfless, altruistic quests of virtue.

That was what was fed to the common people, but Varro—growing up in the slums of the Suburro district—had scoffed at the notion even in his youth.

"Yes, yes, you are right," Varro said. "It is true."

Some emperors, apparently, believed in the grand delusions they were selling. The Empire, lending support to its allies with only their good in mind. It was a statement worthy of a jester, entertaining the rabble in Imperial Square.

The annoyance on Seánus' face faded, and he extended his hand. He was once again in that majestic domed chamber of white marble.

"Our northern border is being guarded with the help of the Second Anthanian Legion, and with the help of our brave legionaries, it has been almost entirely sealed off.

"Trade with the Eastern Kingdoms has intensified, and with the colony of Bregantium, and with the aid of our public servants new routes have been discovered to Seshán and beyond. The Empire, in two-hundred-and-tenth year since the Unification, has never been stronger, our people never more secure and prosperous. Soon Anthania Province will be free from war and unrest, and the peace will endure forever."

But Varro knew peace was a fragile thing, and that in this

world, it never lasted long.

"An excellent job," he said, and this time there was no deceit in his lips. It was among the better performances Varro had seen, and Emperor Seánus, who had served in war, was convincing in his role.

But the emperor's eyes were weary. He was still bothered, still undone. He seemed shrunken by what had happened to Julia, reduced as a human being. As for his daughter, she was likely dead; but he had no way to bury her, no way to honor her like her ancestors had been honored.

Tragedies fell upon even the Seáni. "He holds the stars in his hands" indeed.

~

At times, when the emperor was gone and there was no need to protect him, Varro would return to the old haunt.

He passed through Julia's bedchamber and saw that all was still in place, the great window overlooking the hill and the hippodrome below. He stepped through the shattered glass, through the balustrade, into the light that was shining through the window and reflecting on yellow curtains.

Glinting glass, an empty feeling, all of it was the same, and it grew more and more haunting every time Varro returned. As the Marshal of the Guard, it was his duty to search for her… but where could she be? Where could she have gone?

~

It was raining when Varro returned to the broken up fence. Just beyond it was an abandoned, dilapidated building, and old crumbling apartment blocks where animals had taken up residence. The fence looked down on the smoky valley of the Suburro, Varro's childhood home, the city's poorest and most notorious district. Could answers lie there, in that squalid place? Varro would soon find out.

Chapter Six

Tidus Sulpicius Varro, Marshal of the Guard

Down the road ventured, down, down, down, in a valley between the Equine and Aurean Hills, to a place where the smoke of smithies and the stench of tanneries settled. It was Imperial City's most populous section, where the dockhands of Imperial Harbor and the street musicians of Imperial Square could afford to live.

The apartment blocks were so high they crowded out the sky. The sides of the tuff concrete buildings were stained by smoke and ash. And when Varro walked—having discarded his armor and clothed himself in the attire of a commoner—he brushed shoulders no matter where he stepped. So many people there were, like schools of sardines swarming through the Imperial Harbor or the Bay of Nichaeus. It was dark as well, for the smoke was omnipresent, and the light of the sun was faint—though its heat had only increased.

People live here, Varro thought in awe, but then he remembered he also once lived here, in a small shanty home on Straight Street. That was where he had been brought up; that was where he had answered the call of his country, joined the First Seldanian Legion and scaled up the ranks to where he was today.

It was still shocking to see that this great valley, covered in soot, was so close to the ostentation and wealth of the Imperial Palace. It was the place where the poor lived, where the destitute holed up in dark and dismal rooms, where poverty and crime reigned. Had the emperor's daughter been taken here? The thought was almost humorous to him, blue-blooded Julia Seánus in her silken gown, too dainty to kill a spider on her own, walking amid these seedy streets.

But it wasn't funny, Varro realized. It wasn't funny at all.

His smirk faded into a frown as he questioned himself, as he questioned his surroundings.

It was hard to get a gander at it all, and as he stood there in the middle of the road, dozens and dozens of people brushed by him. And the late spring air converged, the mélange of smells seemed to coalesce into one miasma, the refuse, the garbage, the excreta and the smell of the tanneries, the unbathed and unwashed Suburro denizens. He reminded himself, despite his disgust, that he had once been one of these people; he once lived among this squalor. A long time ago, he had been a resident of the Suburro, and the Suburro was still in him; the Suburro was still in his heart. It was where he had been raised, where he had grown up, where he had been forged in a dark crucible. This place was a part of him; it always would be, no matter where his military career took him.

Through the roaring crowd, past yapping dogs and groups of children, Varro pushed himself down the way, and it all came back to him, how one had to assert himself to get by here. There was no polite waiting, no courtesy, just the rough-and-tumble of the Suburro, the dark streets, the foul scents, the illicit entertainments.

The road eventually broke away into a moderately sized square, and there, there was some breathing room, a little space to stand. An ox cart was driving through, carrying with it piles of amphorae, clay jars no doubt full of wine. The sun was at its maximum extent, and the pavestones were gleaming. Ahead of him, just ahead, on the perimeter of the square overlooking Potters' Street, there was a tavern, multi-storied, built off the face of one of the apartment blocks. At the street level, at outdoor tables, there were assorted Suburro denizens drinking wine, and beyond them, a great oaken double door that was open. Varro needed to get out of this heat, out of these swarming crowds. He checked to see if his sword was still in its sheath. It was dangling from his belt.

He knew just how dangerous the taverns of Suburro could be. But he needed a little rest, to collect his thoughts, to focus, to breathe. If he was going to spend the day searching, he needed to be calm and methodical, not frenzied.

~

The tavern was dark inside, and on the marble floors there were rugs to walk on, and springs of aloe and lavender to improve the smell. On a stage in the far back corner, lit by colored lamps, were a piper, a lutist, and a singer. There was also a dancer who was twirling this way and that with a length of red cloth in her hand.

"Signore!" A voice snapped him from his thoughts.

The innkeeper was there, a woman with long black hair, two dark eyes and a gown of scarlet. Her skin was sumptuous and well-cared for, a pallid white.

"Welcome to the Tavern of the Red Lord," she said. "I am Maria. Maria Domina, they call me."

"A pleasure," Varro said. "May I have a seat?"

"Of course," Maria answered, and, crossing the room, clutched Varro's fist with a cold hand. "The Inner Room is all for you."

Maria led him down a narrow path through tables and chairs. The room was mostly empty, but eventually she led him beyond dark red curtains, into a shady room. Within the room was a table and about a dozen chairs. Facing the table, on the other side of the room, a symbol was painted on the wall, a dark red handprint. Varro wondered just what it was, if it had to do with religion or with some secret society. He felt faint.

"I—" he began but before he could finish servants appeared behind him, helping him into his chair. The sprigs of lavender and aloes were pungent, erasing all trace of foulness, but they were sharp, and his head began to ache. The servants helped him to his seat, and moments later ,more servants came, bringing him a goblet of wine. The wine was a dark red, and flowers and bits of fruit were floating within it. There were ice shavings within it as well. Ice, in Imperial City, was taken from the mountains and stored in underground cellars. Did this tavern have an ice chamber? If so, there had to be more to it than was let on, a deep underground part hidden from the eye.

"I'll pay…" he began.

"No payment," Maria said. "This is a specialty of the house. We will have you drink it. We will be by to see if you have need of anything."

But as he was left alone in the Inner Room, he thought twice about drinking of the goblet. He began to question everything. He dipped his finger in the cold wine, finding it icy to the touch. He took the goblet in his hands and smelled the liquid up close, allowing its pungent scent to pierce his nose. But he detected nothing. White powder, night root, they all had a certain scent to them, one that the trained could discern.

What was he thinking? Why would Maria want to harm him? Why would any of them want to harm him? They were just being hospitable.

And yet he set the goblet down and did not drink it. His eyes returned to the wall across from him, painted with the dark handprint. He wondered what it meant.

He tried to stamp it in his mind, to remember its contours, its exact method of painting. He noted in the center of the hand was lighter than the perimeter.

He eyed the goblet, and eyed the white flower petals floating like islands in a sea of red. It was tempting, but he was not here for pleasure. He saw that there was a bell in the center of the table, and he took it, and rang it.

An attendant came running in. "Yes, signore? I am at your service!"

Varro pointed to the symbol, painted in such clear, dark ink on the wall opposite him. "What does that mean?" he said.

The attendant's face brightened; her eyes widened. "The Order of the Red Hand." In a moment's span she had changed, speaking with the zeal of a proselyte. "Do you wish to learn more?"

Varro suddenly didn't. This had nothing to do with the disappearance of the Empire's princess; it would bring him no closer to Julia.

The spring heat had gotten to him; what was he doing here, anyway?

"I will meet you after dark," the attendant said. "Outside… I will tell you more."

"No," Varro said. "That's all right."

~

After getting his bearings, Varro scoured the streets of the Suburro. He picked through all the ground he could cover, passing twice by his old family home—and seeing that it was in the possession of a new tenant.

But as for Julia, he had not heard a word; and among the guards of the urban cohort on duty, they claimed to have seen nothing. There were no sightings of Julia Ultima anywhere; and so Varro relinquished his quest for now.

He returned to the Imperial Palace as the sun was setting, as light glanced over the rooftops, and thoughts of Maria and the Order of the Red Hand percolated. Today's search had been fruitless, leaving only that troubling memory.

Chapter Seven

Achiba

The keep of Eioli was built deep beneath the earth, and as Achiba ventured down a set of steps, he noted their antiquity. The stairs heading downwards were worn away and marbled by time, the walls and ceilings crudely chiseled. The stone of the Ugar Coast was soft and easy to work, but still, as he passed great vaults and sprawling chambers he couldn't help but marvel.

His mother was not the only woman heading downwards; only women, and children like Achiba, would hide away during such serious times. The men, all above their fourteenth year, were expected to stay and fight, to hold off the Imperial siege to their last breath. Achiba thought of his father, fighting the Imperial dogs with bravery, and at that thought his heart began to race, worrying that he'd lose him forever.

"Hurry!" Mother said as another boulder fell on the city high above, and the ground shook as if an earthquake had struck.

Deep below the earth, the stairs eventually ended, and there in a great chamber of impossible size were the city's women and children, thousands and thousands in number, countless like the sand of the seashore. And before them was the statue of the great god Belpheor, forged of the same rock as the keep, his horns jutting out from his head, a ring in his nose. Before that statue was an altar caked with dried blood, where the goats and pigs of many years had been split open on the rock.

Though it was stone, the sight of Belpheor made Achiba queasy. It was so lifelike, so very lifelike. Achiba half expected it to, at an inopportune moment, stand up and murder those gathered there. Worse, the statue's eyes seemed to follow you wherever they went, though they were chiseled of stone, as lifeless as the body itself.

Mother led Achiba and his siblings to the corner of the room. The keep was cold and damp, and though they were deep beneath the earth, the sound of battle was still audible, boulders pummeling the ground and the distant shouts of warriors rising into the night.

He recalled the time before the war, as the Empire advanced throughout the peninsula, hearing of city after city becoming "Friends"—that is, slaves—of the Empire. The Empire turned the cities of the coast against one another. They divided the Ugars just as they had divided prior enemies. Eioli was the only free city left, the only city that dared to stand up to the Empire's might, the only city that dared to make its own way. The Empire forced the Ugars to worship foreign gods and reject the ones they revered. The Empire replaced the cities' kings with puppets. They were dogs, through and through, worthy only of scorn. Only Eioli remained free. Only Eioli refused to bend the knee.

"Damned Imperials," Mother said, and handed blankets to Achiba's younger siblings.

Despite her best efforts, Mother's fear was peeking through, and beyond her stern look her face was pallid, almost white.

A priest was making his way through the crowd, and women and children backed away from him in fear. His lavender robe was brilliant, and the staff in his wizened hands was twisted and knobby. His eyes were dark black, inky almost, and on his head was a great purple-and-green headdress gleaming with tiny crystals. He was flanked by two guards bearing swords.

The priest knelt before the altar, then fell prostrate, and his robe was like a great sea, filling the area around the statue.

Mother drew backward and put a hand on Achiba's head.

She was muttering curses. She said, "Stay away."

But her voice was loud enough for the priest to hear, and the priest turned his eyes to look at them. He rose up from his prostrate position and as he walked toward them, began to smile.

"Do not listen to your mother, little Achiba," the priest said. "Do not stay away from me, for in Belpheor is our only hope."

The priest was drawing near him, getting closer and closer with each step.

How did the priest know his name? All names were recorded in the temple, all births, marriages and deaths. But faces were not.

"Achiba," the priest said when he had almost crossed the room, when he was within touching distance. "Come with me!"

"Stay away from him!" Mother howled and charged forward. The guards shouted and drew spears and shields, bolting over to them. But Mother fell back, and the priest's eyes returned to Achiba, gazing upon him, examining him.

"You," the priest said. "You are young. Your mind is like soft clay; it can be worked, and smoothed over, and baked. You are coming with me."

"No!" Mother wailed, and this time she truly charged, but the soldiers caught her, preventing all movement.

Could Achiba say no to a priest? In the society of the Ugars, priests were higher than nobility, higher than any person besides the king.

"Come with me," the priest said. "That is an order from Belpheor himself."

~

Achiba followed the priest up the steps, out through the double doors, into the night air. It was pitch dark and the sounds of battle had faded. No boulders fell; no fires raged. There were shouts in the distance, on the walls, but it had faded with the night, and the moon had arisen—pale and white—and clouds wisped the sky. The Ugar Coast was on the cusp of summer, but Achiba was not excited.

The priest led him down a dark street. Achiba's hands were clammy; they were shaking. He wondered what the priest wanted. He wanted to be gone from him, to sprint back down into the keep. But he knew if he valued his life he had to keep going, to give this priest whatever he wanted, to listen, to obey. He knew the cruelty of the priests; he knew what schemers they were that lived in the temple. Even the king feared the priesthood.

"Tell me, Achiba," the priest said. "Do you love Belpheor?"

The answer was no. He thought nothing of the city's god, and the statues of him, placed in sacred parts of the city, tended to terrify him. Mother never spoke of him, nor father; they told him to keep away from priests and the Consecrated Ones.

But he lied, for he feared what the priest would do if he told the truth. "Yes," Achiba answered. "I do. I do love Belpheor."

A boulder came thundering down in the distance, and there was a great crash as a house collapsed. Far in the distance, at the city walls, the men of the city were like ants on an anthill. They would keep their watch all night, as the moon made her skyward journey, as the stars moved by in their royal procession.

The priest stopped his walk before a great statue: Belpheor, with the head of a bull and the body of a man, terrified Achiba as always, but more fearsome was he than ever at night, and night it was. The statue's eyes were lifelike, seeming to peer into Achiba though they were of stone. He could not bear to look at it, and so he turned to the priest, and found the priest's dark eyes no less comforting.

"You will make a good servant of Belpheor, little Achiba," the priest said.

Achiba did not want to be a priest; it was the last thing he wanted, the last thing he desired.

But for the sake of his safety he decided to listen, to pretend he wanted to hear what the priest had to say.

The priest was smiling. "When I was little, I didn't want to be a servant either. My mother tried to halt Belpheor's call. 'You will not have my Drubal,' she would say. But her Drubal became the chief priest."

Achiba had heard all he wanted to. But he knew he could not go back. He would have to wriggle his way out of this situation, with all the cunning and cleverness he could come up with.

"Let me tell you a secret, little Achiba," Drubal said. "It is all a fraud… everything you heard, everything you learned, all these statues. It is all falsehood."

"What do you mean?" Achiba said.

"In great days, in the times of the ancients, our lord Belpheor would hear our call," Drubal said. "He would drive against our enemies… he would spread panic in the ranks of armies. He would cause plague and rain down pestilence.

"And for a long time, it was so. But his power began to fade, though the oxen's blood was spilled, though pigs and horses were flayed upon the altar. And soon, it was as if he was asleep. He would respond to nothing, nothing at all. If all the blood in the world were sprayed upon the altar, still he would not answer. Our god is powerless. He was asleep. Now he is dead!"

Such honesty was remarkable, but it did not comfort Achiba. He turned to see the raging battle, and saw that the flaming boulder had caught another part of the city on fire. They were doomed; they were all doomed. The Ugars would be no more—at least, those Ugars who refused to become slaves, "Friends" of the Empire. The cities of the coast had fallen down in submission, all cities except Eioli, the one city that chose to fight.

"But he can be stirred to life!" Drubal said. "And you can help us. I know you can."

Achiba did not want to be a priest; he wanted no part in the ritual. But perhaps he had no choice.

Chapter Eight

Tidus Sulpicius Varro, Marshal of the Guard

Varro watched from the shadows as the emperor addressed the Imperial Council.

The thirty old men, all belonging to the August class, were as blueblooded as the emperor himself.

Varro was a Knight, the lesser of the two tiers of nobility, but he was still above the common. His grandfather was the breaking point for the Varro family; he had fallen on hard times, and so his descendants had been forced to live and subsist in the Suburro. The noble title hadn't helped them with anything; in Imperial City, money mattered more than all else. Money was the highest distinction, and they'd never had any.

From the shadows he watched as the emperor began to speak. Varro could tell he was nervous; the emperor, who commanded the Empire's armies, was vulnerable only to these thirty old men, these Councilors. For they had it in their power to remove him by unanimous vote; and it was in their hands that the Empire's finances were controlled. They were in charge of the purse strings; when united, their power was unequalled.

"Men of the Imperial Council… distinguished citizens all…"

Varro remembered this speech. The emperor had rehearsed it to him.

"I bring you news good and bad from the far corners."

Ah, yes, good and bad. Varro had heard this tripe already; he recalled every word, and the manner in which it was said.

"The campaign in the barbarian coastlands is approaching its end. The Fourth Peregothian Legion lies encamped around the last rebel city, Eioli, and Legate Lentulus has been entrusted with seeing the mission to its conclusion. But as we increase our grip in the cities of Ugarit let us remember our calling, that the Empire seeks no conquests or dominations, but only to support our allies."

The line that Varro almost laughed at was met with stony silence by the Imperial Council. Old faces they were, as if carved of stone, steely-eyed, white-haired. Varro had never seen them laugh while in session, or even crack a smile. They were ever somber, ever serious. They were the oldest, the wisest of the Empire, or so they claimed; they were the elders, Augusts all.

"Bad news remains," the emperor continued. "There is unrest in the city below us, yes, unrest. We have doubled the size of the urban cohorts and have begun to arrest Red Hand members."

Varro couldn't believe what he had heard. The Order of the Red Hand… that was what the girl in that tavern had tried to recruit him for. What was the order, he wondered, and why did it rise to the level of a crime? In the Empire, liberty was one of the chief virtues, and only the violent were arrested.

"The situation in the streets is being taken care of," the emperor said. "As always, I have the utmost faith in the men of our legions, those brave souls who take up the cause of our country."

"And do not forget about yourself." The words of Agatho, the Speaker of the Council, silenced the emperor suddenly. "You must care for yourself, Your Excellency. You must allow yourself to grieve."

"Grieve?" The emperor was no longer in that state of trance, no longer giving a speech. "I will not grieve. Julia is alive. I know it."

The poor sap. Varro supposed it was good for him to cling to hope.

"And this man… this man is tasked with finding her…"

When the emperor gestured to Varro, he felt like a bug exposed to sunlight, after a child removed a rock from the cold damp earth. He was not meant for sunlight; he did not like attention, not by any means, and he did not want it. But nonetheless Varro stepped forward, onto the marble floor. Sunlight was shining in through the dome's oculus above; it sparkled on his armor.

Varro inclined his head to the Speaker of the Council; though he was, by law, their inferior, it was so difficult for him to bow. It was not in his nature.

"And you… the Marshal of the Guard… the emperor has given his report about our nation. What about your task, which is no less important?"

What could he tell them? What would he venture to? He had learned a little, but he had kept so much to himself. Staggered by the unexpected attention, he began to stammer: "I… I… the necklace…"

"What? What do you mean?" the Speaker of the Council said.

Perhaps, he was so skilled at questioning, so skilled at examining witnesses, he'd managed to scare the truth out of Varro.

"I… I…" Varro was beside himself. "There is a breach in the fence… a place where the commoners can draw near the Imperial Palace. I found her necklace there… it was broken."

"Why didn't you tell me this?" the emperor cried. "We've lost time! Bring the necklace to me at once! Where is it?"

"I will be back," Varro said.

~

The star gem in the middle of the necklace glittered. The sunlight, pouring in from the Council House's oculus, caused it to radiate and sparkle.

The emperor strode over, took it in his hands. "This… this…" His eyes were watering. "A family heirloom. The Star of Seladora. She would not leave it behind willingly. It was ripped from her."

It seemed reality had dawned on him, but what Varro was really thinking about, what he was really concerned for, was what he had unleashed. He had kept the matter quiet; now the whole palace would know. Everything that the Imperial Council was told was eventually widely known; they were loose lipped, and this nest of vipers would know what Varro knew.

Julia could not have been abducted without the knowledge of someone inside the palace; and whatever twisted viper had done that to her would be alerted now.

All because of those dark, examining eyes, the whole mission had been compromised, all because of the Speaker's line of questioning. It was a travesty.

"How long have you known about this?" the emperor said.

"Tell no one," Varro said, then looked at the assembled council. "Tell no one!"

Chapter Nine

Publius Allius Corvus

The mountains were vast and to Publius, ascending them was exhausting. These mountains, called the Easthorns, were in the northern part of the peninsula called Anthania. The towering peaks, some still covered in snow, were surrounded by forests of thick black pines. The darkness was deep, even during the day, and Publius began to feel claustrophobic, cramped, trapped. His training in the hill country to the south had gotten him accustomed to the wide open sky, to seeing the horizon from one end to the other, to wispy white clouds floating through a crystal blue firmament. Storm clouds were abovehead; there was a sharp spear of lightning, followed instantly by thunder. Then a drizzle began, cold splashes of water on Publius' neck. They were ill prepared for storms, though the storms seemed to come at the same time each evening.

The centurion leading them was a man named Caro, a long time veteran whose roots were in the island of Seldanis. Yet as the days progressed and turned into weeks, up the winding mountain roads, Publius began to quietly suspect that things were not as they seemed; he became even more doubtful that the Second Anthanian Legion was posted in these mountains. Though there were silver mines and iron mines to protect, there didn't seem to be any threat to them. The barbarians were to the north, and across the sea; the Easthorns were entirely contained within the Empire's territory. So why would the emperor, in his great wisdom, post the most famous legion here, where there was no need for protection, no need for sword or shield?

The daylight was waning, and the darkness was setting in. A cold and bracing wind blew as Caro stopped his jog and signaled to the thirteen recruits that it was time to halt for the day. On the lonely mountain road, amid the driving wind and rain, the recruits began to assemble their tents. The air was thin and cold.

Near the road, a cliff overlooked a deep valley; in the distance was a grand peak, a jagged wonderwork of stone capped in snow. They were so far from civilization it defied description; they were truly in the middle of the wilderness, with no one to help if they ever fell into danger.

"Prepare a fire," Caro said, looking at Publius, and Publius nodded his head.

He wandered into the midst of the forest, into the forest floor scattered with sticks. He needed kindling to burn.

~

He was in the darkness of the woods, far from camp, bundling twigs and fallen branches in his arms. Creating a fire in the rain would be almost impossible, but they had done it before, with exceptional hard work and exceptional equipment. A cold wind was blowing through the trees, and the boughs of the pines were wafting in the wind.

In the distance he heard a cry, like the cry of a woman. He dropped the kindling he'd collected and drew his sword, charging in the direction of the voice.

He ran through the forest, past rocks and springs and flowing streams.

He heard a shout from the distance, a voice he recognized: "Publius!"

Publius turned to see Caro standing there.

"I… I thought I heard a woman's voice," Publius said.

"A woman's voice?" Caro said. "You're hearing things, Publius." There was a mocking smile on his face. "Although you're not alone. The Woman of the Mountain is a famous legend."

"The Woman of the Mountain?" Publius said.

"She is said to call after those who are about to die," Caro said.

As the fire burned, and the embers glowed red among the raging flame, Publius rubbed his hands at the warmth, and pondered how he had gotten here, and why. He had been born poor, in one of the most impoverished places in Imperial City; and yet he had had something going for him in his youth, that his father was a craftsman of full rank, a tailor more than capable of providing for his family.

His father had given Publius' elder brother the family business, yes; but in a true sense he had chosen this path for himself. Yes, he had chosen to be a soldier. Though his path had been limited, though he was no man of means, he had decided this for himself. He had admired the soldiers he'd seen in the streets of Imperial City. He had wondered at them, at their helmets— gleaming, silvery iron, with broad red horsehair crests. He had believed their tales of patriotism.

But now… now, high in the mountains, trapped with these dozen souls, he had begun to doubt his path. He had begun to doubt everything, about the way he had chosen, about the soldier's life, even the Empire, that he had loved.

He had learned of the Empire's new war against the Ugars, how every city, every single city, had agreed to become subservient allies—every city except one, Eioli. And with ruthlessness and bloodthirst the Empire had set itself against this Eioli. The last Publius heard from Caro, Eioli had held firm, longer than any city before it. The Ugars were not as primitive as Imperials thought.

And he had had dreams, yes, Publius had had dreams. Ever since they ascended to the mountains, ever since they ventured onto its winding paths, he had awoken—sometimes in the middle of the night—panting and full of fear. And when he marched, there was anxiety in his heart, though he did not know why. He felt as if they were marching toward something terrible, but he did not know what it was.

He eyed the recruits huddled around the fire. He thought of the voices in the woods.

He did not know why, but he rose up, and Caro looked at him questioningly. The moon was out, and the stars were shining brilliantly, gleaming pinpoints of light. There was enough light to move around, enough space to breathe. It was night, but he could manage.

"I'll be right back," Publius said, and stood up. He ventured off into the woods, into the darkness, the darkness where he had heard the voice.

The wan moonlight shone upon the snow. The pine boughs were laden with white. The air was crisp, as cold as it was thin.

He did not want to be with Caro, or with the green recruits he was shepherding. He had come to realize, at long last, that he did not trust him.

And there was a figure far off, wreathed in shadow. He focused his eyes, and saw a woman in a thick fur coat. Her hair was blonde, her eyes blue as sapphires. She was lingering there amid the snow. The air was still; there was not a trace of wind. The snowy peaks created a vast canvas above. They were at the roof of the world, at the height of the unspoiled mountains, utterly alone.

Was this the woman he had heard? Was this the Woman of the Mountain that Caro had spoken of?

Her lips were luscious, and though the air was cold there was no trace of blue or purple to them. Her eyes were like glistening orbs, and the richness of her furs only made her seem more out of place. She was like a wealthy woman walking the streets of Imperial City in winter; a woman who did not belong among the wilds.

Her lips began to move; she spoke. "Come here!" she said.

Publius recalled the legends he had heard, of spirits who would meet you in a fatal embrace, and drain the life from you. Yet what was worse? Caro, or that?

"What do you want from me?" Publius said.

The woman smiled; the moon reflected on her luscious lips.

She was beautiful, Publius noted.

"Come here!" she said again, and at that moment he realized this voice was indeed the one he had heard before. "I must tell you something!"

"What do you want to tell me?" Publius said.

"Draw near me," she said. "it is a matter of life and death."

But Publius stood still, refusing to move, refusing to turn.

"If you must tell me something," Publius said, "say it now."

The woman hesitated, as if disappointed. "Great things are at work, Publius, things you do not understand. Things that shall not alter just the Empire but eternity."

It was a strange thing, a madwoman in the snow, fair of form, but speaking nonsense. She was out of place.

In response to her nonsensical words, Publius kept silent. He stared into her blue eyes. She was beautiful.

"Turn back," the woman said. "Turn back, Publius. This mountain is evil. Run while you still have a chance."

Publius, she had said. She knew his name.

He tried to speak again, but snow began to fall, and like a curtain the flakes hid her. The wind was blowing again.

Publius pondered whether he should follow after her, whether he should heed her advice, but in the end he turned, heading back to camp.

Chapter Ten

Tidus Sulpicius Varro, Marshal of the Guard

The days following Varro's admission had been pure pandemonium.

From his room's balcony he surveyed the city below, paying special attention to the Suburro.

Smoke was wafting up from the decrepit district, the dumping ground of the city's poor.

The streets of the city had been militarized, and now the urban cohorts were combing through house and shop alike, seeking information on Julia's disappearance.

It was everything Varro feared, everything he dreaded. It had all come true. Now, not only the Imperial Palace had been notified—not just that nest of vipers—but common citizens as well. Whoever had taken Julia, whoever had abducted her, would now know what Varro had learned. The sawed-off part of the fence had now been repaired, and guards were posted everywhere.

There was a knock on Varro's door.

"Come in!" he shouted.

Standing there was Thedus, his second-in-command, the Master of the Shield. In the pecking order of the Imperial Guard, only Varro was superior to him.

"I thought you were on duty," Varro said.

"The emperor has gone to bed."

It was only an hour past noon.

"I think," Thedus said, "that his grief has finally caught up with him. He must deal with the grief as best he knows how."

The Empire's struggles would continue, with or without its figurehead.

"Grief can be debilitating," Varro said. "He has more to

answer to than himself, more than Julia. The functioning of the state depends on him."

"And yet, he has withdrawn himself, Varro," Thedus said. "He is beginning to succumb."

"Why are you here, Thedus?" Varro said.

Thedus pursed his lips. He reached into the folds of his pocket and produced a scroll. It was sealed with a red wax seal. "The castellan said this is for you. He told me to give it to you."

Varro walked over and took the scroll in his hand. He punctured the seal with his finger and unraveled the letter. The ink was dark black, with perfectly shaped letters.

> *Varro, Marshal of the Guard:*
> *It was a pleasure to have your company.*
> *But there is unfinished business. I know who you are looking for.*
> *I know where she is.*
> *Yours,*
> *Maria Domina*

There was no indication of her location, but Varro instantly knew who it was. This was the lady from the tavern, the lady who had offered him the glass of wine.

It was the tavern where he'd been told of the Order of the Red hand.

He gasped and took a step back.

He knew he could not ignore this; he knew he had to follow wherever this led him.

Maria Domina was not a woman he had wanted to meet again; but he needed to speak to her, right away. He would pry the knowledge from her lips, one way or another.

Varro found himself staring into Thedus' eyes blankly. He was wary of telling him too much, wary of letting him in on what he knew. He had, already, been careless with his words, and with disastrous results. Now the whole city knew of Julia's broken necklace; the whole city knew what had gone on.

~

Flanked by three guards on either side, Varro marched from the Imperial Palace into the slums of the Suburro.

He no longer looked on it with saccharine memories, but instead with the hard edge of truth. He glared at the impoverished souls shambling to and fro; he scowled at the dirty streets, full of mud and garbage. And he pressed on with his goals, heading straight on his path, until he came to the doors of the tavern.

He noted for the first time, the words written above the door: "The Tavern of the Red Lord."

He tried the knob and found it wouldn't budge. He cursed under his breath, and consecrating his action to the god Imperium, he took to work, kicking relentlessly until the wood splintered, and the hinges buckled, and the door fell with a great crash.

The tavern was dark. "Maria Domina!" he called out.

There were no oil lamps to illuminate the room, just gloom. But there was a figure running away, a glimmer of cloth.

"You!" Varro cried. "Stop right there!"

But she had slipped down through one of the side rooms, and Varro gave chase.

The Tavern of the Red Lord was dark and unlit. Varro ordered his underlings to fetch a light, and not long after they produced an oil lamp that glowed brightly.

Maria Domina… she had teased him with that letter, but Varro would not be teased.

His men followed him with the lamp, and one by one he scoured the rooms, finding them empty, as if the tavern had been abandoned. It was not yet sunset, and besides, taverns kept open late into the night.

Through his position as Marshal of the Guard, Varro had been granted the authority of Imperium.

"By the power of the Empire," Varro said, "I seize this tavern and put it in the keeping of the state!"

His words had purchase; barring action by the magistrates, the Tavern of the Red Lord was in the State's possession, and he could dismantle it bit by bit.

But there was no trace of anyone, and Varro began to question himself. He began to question whether he had really seen anyone at all.

The Tavern of the Red Lord. What a strange name.

He knew some taverns were fronts for criminal enterprises, or places where thieves sold fenced goods. In the Suburro, the most lawless part of Imperial City, the reach of justice was strained, and crime went largely unanswered. But Varro had made an oath; he had promised the emperor that—by any means necessary—he would find his daughter. Dead or alive he would find her; wounded, maimed, or well.

That night they dismantled the entire tavern. They searched for any sign of Julia.

They went to the temple registry, seeing the names of the citizens who had been born throughout the centuries; but no trace of one named Maria Domina could be found.

Chapter Eleven

Tidus Sulpicius Varro, Marshal of the Guard

In the morning, Varro stood guard over the emperor as he ate his morning meal. He was dining with his ministers, with the Magister of Food and Wine, the Magister of Public Works, and more.

The sting of his failure lingered, and as Varro eyed the emperor, he seemed reduced. The grief had finally arrived. He was in control of the Empire, of the whole of the nation, but he was not just a figurehead; he was a human as well.

The magisters were speaking of the war against the Ugars.

"I never wanted this war," the emperor said. "I was forced into it."

It had not gone as they had hoped. Months later and—as far as the Imperial government had heard—the city of Eioli held fast. Worse, their bravery against the legion was inspiring the other cities of the Ugar Coast. "Friends of the Empire" they were, for now, but perhaps not long afterward. That tenuous alliance of the defeated had begun showing signs of wear.

As the morning meal began to vanish from the table—pickled eggs, cured ham, puddings and sweetbreads and roasts—the emperor's eyes met Varro's. Varro looked away, not wishing to engage.

But soon the meal was ended.

"Come with me," the emperor said.

~

The majesty of the Imperial bedchamber was one that never failed to amaze you; it was breathtaking in scale, the size of many taverns, with a great main hall in the center. It was bright white, faced with marble, with gold urns everywhere, and paintings of the countryside hanging on the walls. The curtains of the windows were of silk, and the windows themselves were forged of ribbed glass. Aloes and fragrant flowers were freshly lain upon the colorful rugs. And it overlooked the sea, the great and vast sea. The sun was shining on the whitecaps, and the Imperial Harbor below bustled with life. Oh, to have a chamber like this, overlooking the city, to keep one's eyes on your inferiors, to have attendants catering to your every need.

But the position of emperor was a tenuous one, and few lasted more than ten years. Pushed out, through force or popular dissent, the Imperial Palace was a shifting turntable, a place where one never was for long.

The emperor beckoned Varro, and together they ventured to the balcony, out through a glass window into the fresh, warm air.

The noise of the city was distant; only a balcony separated them from a drop of many fathoms.

Varro began to think longingly of his career in the legions, how, in spare and meager conditions, he had avoided all this avarice and ambition. The palace behind him was a nest of vipers, a den of conniving and conspiracies, a place where honor was laughed at and duty was scorned.

The emperor turned to Varro amid the smoky air, and to Varro's surprise the emperor's eyes had welled with tears. He was on the verge of crying.

"She is dead," the emperor said. "She is dead. I know it."

"How could you know it?" Varro said.

Varro did not know how to comfort people; it was certainly not one of his gifts. Showing any sign of emotion in the legion was an invitation to mockery and scorn.

And yet he touched the emperor's shoulder.

"There, there," he said, and winced as soon as he said the

words. "You do not know… no one knows… and from what little time I spent with Julia, I know she is wise beyond her years. If anyone will survive capture, she will."

"Ah, Varro." The emperor's voice had grown faint. "If I told you something secret, would you swear not to repeat it? Would you swear it on Lorenus? On all the gods?"

"I will swear it on my martial honor," Varro said.

It was, after all, the thing he held most sacred. The rituals, the throngs of worshippers, the marbled temples and the pillared colonnades, those things were not close to his heart. But the honor of the legion was still in him, and honor was the foundation of his life.

The emperor strode out, slumped downward, grabbing hold of the balcony. The daylight was shining on the hazy streets, and the smoke of the buildings caused the sun to glare. The summer months were almost upon them.

"Say this to no one else," the emperor began, "for I have told no one. Only my wife knows of this."

There was a long pause, and the sounds of the city below formed one low cacophony. In the crystalline harbor ships were darting to and fro.

"I know she is dead," the emperor said, "because I do not see her anymore."

"You do not see her?" Varro said. "Your wife is not here with us. Is she dead as well?"

The emperor grumbled something under his breath. "No, no, Varro, you do not understand," Varro said. "You have not witnessed what I have. You see, ever since my daughter was a little girl, she had a special talent. She would appear to me at all hours of the night, and then vanish; and then, when I returned to the nursery, I would see here there in her crib, giggling, all alone."

"What are you talking about?" Varro said.

"My daughter had a talent," the emperor said. "One that I

think even she did not understand. She called what she did 'projection.' She could appear in places—not physically, but in the mind—and then vanish just as quickly. She could speak to me from afar.

"I tried to find a teacher to instruct her in this gift, but the augurs and the flamens had never seen anything like what Julia could do. There was no sorcerer with similar powers in history.

"So she taught herself, Varro, and as she taught herself she grew stronger, and her skill was more developed. Soon she could appear, in her astral form, to people far away, to places she'd never been to, to persons she had never met. When I was on the military campaigns, she would project herself, appearing to me in her absence, and every night I would hear from her…"

Varro had begun inching away.

"You see, Varro, call my daughter an augur, call her a sorceress, but she had a keen talent, one she had honed throughout her adolescence. And ever since the night she disappeared, I have not heard from her, not a single word. She is dead, and I have no way to bury her."

At the emperor's words, Varro did not know what to say. He didn't want to say anything. He wondered what had caused this madness in him, if the grief—which he had suppressed for the sake of the nation—had caused him to imagine these things.

Projection… astral bodies… it was madness. Sure, all humans had spirits, but their spirits were tied to their bodies. What the emperor was talking about was nonsense.

"Keep up your hope," Varro said, dreaming of a way to end this conversation. "The gods are with your daughter. They loved her."

It was the best he could think of, and as he spoke the saccharine words he winced twice as much as he had when he had patted the emperor's shoulder.

"I know they did," the emperor said. "I know they did."

Chapter Twelve

Achiba

The temple of Belpheor, leering high above the city of Eioli, was a place that struck fear into the heart of Achiba from a very early age. He did not know what the priests did up there, but it was omnipresent, an architectural horror of bare spires and harsh angles. It was visible from every point in the city, and people would speak of it only in hushed tones.

Yet in the morning, as the battle began anew, Achiba found himself walking up the ramp. The High Priest, Drubal, was leading him to the very place he feared.

Achiba did not want to be a priest; he did not want to learn the craft. He did not want to strike terror in the hearts of the people of Eioli; most of all, he wanted nothing to do with the sharp, leering statues of the bull-headed god that guarded crossroads. Yet he knew that if he refused, Drubal would have him killed.

As he ascended the ramp, he saw the battle had resumed after the night's brief silence.

Drubal had dressed Achiba in the attire of an acolyte, a white robe that fell to his ankles. Against his will all this was happening; against his will he walked up the steps, as the sound of battle roared below, and as mixed fires throughout the city glowed like beacons. The war had now been raging for three months, but the city of Eioli was well-provided for, having set aside a portion of each harvest. Mother said it would take two years for the Imperials to starve them out; and that was why they were assaulting its walls.

Up, up, up, he walked, and though it was early in the morning, the sun was glaring in its intensity. Summer was almost upon them, the hot and blazing months that sapped the body and the soul.

And then he was there, before the great ceremonial gate marking entrance to the holy place. The gate was flanked by two statues of Belpheor, startling in their lifelike detail, depicting the god with the head of a bull, sitting cross-legged, a finger pointing up to the heavens.

The temple beyond was multistoried, rising in layers toward the sky. Its windows were dark, almost black, and between it in and the ceremonial gate was a great plaza, in the center of which was an altar stained with blood.

"Know, little Achiba," High Priest Drubal said, "that our god is dead; that he no longer hears our cries. And I know why that is, little Achiba. I do. You will change it. You will serve him."

He did not want to serve the god, who every person in Eioli feared; he did not want to join the priests, who struck terror of all who walked the streets. He wanted nothing to do with any of it; but he knew the priesthood was a lifelong calling, and leaving the service meant death.

Achiba followed Drubal down the plaza, his heart racing, his fingers trembling, a cold sweat having broken out all over his body.

I do not want to be here… I do not.

Though he knew he could not escape, he looked this way and that, in some vain hope that somehow, in some manner, he would return to what had been; to where and what he had been before all this happened. His heart cried out for his family, for his sisters, his brother, his mother, his father. He had never wanted this; he had not deserved this. But it had happened to him.

Drubal continued walking across the plaza, and like a lamb to the slaughter Achiba followed him.

Temple Guards were there, wearing iron masks and glittering armor, with spears in their left hands. In unison they laid hold of the double doors and pulled them open. The insides of the temple were lit by torches.

Inside, the wealth of ages was displayed, the money spent from offerings of coin and of blood; golden jars, silver saucers, marble statues over which diamond necklaces and emerald bracelets were laid. There were paintings imported from foreign lands, even from the heathen Empire, hanging on the walls of the white corridors. There were wooden chests filled to the brim with gold coins. And the whole place was thick with the smell of incense and burning resin.

A broad corridor led them deeper into the heart of the temple, and across the stone tiles Achiba walked. There was no turning back. He followed Drubal down the way, past the torches and braziers, past statues of wicked Belpheor.

Drubal turned, and though Achiba did not want to he followed him through a door.

There, in the room, was a glistening pool of water, carved crudely from the earth and layered with green-colored tiles.

"Strip down," Drubal said, "and wash. You must be pure for your service."

Blushing, Achiba unfastened the button from his acolyte's robe and it fell suddenly, baring his naked body. He walked over to the stone steps, and felt the water was refreshing, cold.

He wondered if Drubal could see that he was sweating, that his hands were trembling. It was not good to let a wicked man know you were afraid.

He immersed himself in the water; he brushed his arms and his legs, allowing the liquid to cover him, first his body and then his head. He ran a hand through his hair, stood up, and took a deep breath. He had bathed very little ever since the siege began; but now he was clean, and every breath felt hale.

"Good," Drubal said. "One last impurity remains. Don your robe and follow me."

Achiba waded up through the water, ascended the steps, and crossed the room. He laid the robe of the acolyte over his body, then clasped the button together. He followed Drubal out into the main hallway, amid the flickering torches and lanterns. Past statues he walked, then, through a great door.

There before him was an immense chamber, with the largest statue of Belpheor Achiba had ever seen. So large was it that lamps were placed in its eyeholes, and Achiba screamed and staggered backward.

The priests of the city were there, dozens of them in their dark robes, with miters on their heads. An altar was before the great statue of Belpheor. On the altar was a silver bowl, and in the silver bowl was a hunk of bread.

"Eat," Drubal said and pushed Achiba forward.

Weakly he stepped ahead; he staggered onward, touched the bowl, fumbled with his fingers. The bread was warm to the touch, and had a scent like cinnamon. In his worry, he wondered if it had been poisoned. But he laid hold of it anyway; he pressed it to his lips. He took it, he chewed it, he ate it. It was sweet and wholesome to his tongue.

He turned to Drubal; all fear had fallen away from him. The High Priest was smiling.

"Your service is ended," he said. "Now, you may go back home."

Chapter Thirteen

Tidus Sulpicius Varro, Marshal of the Guard

Maria Domina was nowhere in the city records. No Maria was known to live in the Suburro nor own the Tavern of the Red Lord. The tavern was not listed in city records on the register of businesses; the lot was listed as vacant.

And yet Varro sat there in the palace library, wondering, thinking. He had the registry before him on the table.

The Red Lord… what did that mean, in truth? He got up from his seat.

The library took up an entire wing of the Imperial Palace, and was three floors high. It had the city registries, in addition to books by famed authors and statesmen. It was meant to be a record of the Empire, a record of its histories and its goings on. In some secret chamber there were documents from the Empire's founding, dating to the Unification. But Varro did not have to go that far back to learn of the "Red Lord"—did he?

He had come here at dawn and it was well past noon. He was off duty today; Thedus was charged with the emperor's protection.

Varro rose from his seat, walked past the rows and rows of books, some staggering in height. The spacious chamber was so tightly packed it managed to feel claustrophobic despite its size.

The Red Hand was the name of the cult… was there any record of it in the library? If there was any record of it anywhere, he would find a copy of it here.

He found himself eventually in a dimly lit corner, to a towering shelf crammed with history books. These recorded the goings-on of the Eastern Kingdoms and even the barbarians of the north who were not known for record keeping. But there were also records of foreign religions, of the cults of the Ugars—Belpheor, Daghan, Amman and more.

He picked them up one after the other, scouring them and finding mentions of horrific practices—of human sacrifice, sacred prostitution, and bizarre rituals. But nothing was mentioned of the Red Hand.

Perhaps, even if he found what the Red Hand was, it would not lead him to Maria Domina, who had sent him that letter.

The whole city knew what Varro had found; and perhaps she had had a head start. Perhaps, she had fled the city.

Why, then, would she send him a letter, if she had intended to flee?

If she knew the whereabouts of Julia Seánus, why, then, he would detain her. He would do whatever was required to force that information from her lips. Nothing would be off limits; no method of interrogation would be considered improper or wrong.

He skimmed the books on the religions of the northmen, how they revered the gods of war; how the halflings of the forest worshiped a deity called Peong. But nothing was mentioned of the Red Hand.

He glanced over the books of the southlands, and saw they worshipped the gods of fertility; and in the city of Carta Mega Melkior, the Lord of Precious Things.

But nothing, nothing, nowhere, was a Red Hand mentioned.

Varro had begun to suspect that he would never find the Red Hand. Perhaps it was a folk religion, the province of the simple and the urban poor. There was nothing to be found in the Imperial Library, nothing at all.

So he would have to return to the scene of the crime, and with force to back himself up.

~

With a hundred of the urban cohorts marching behind him, Varro left the fences and towers of the Imperial Palace complex. They marched through the Imperial Square and even the soldiers doing drills took note. The citizens ran away, and the slaves—public and private—did as well. Varro rode at the fore astride a white horse, a sword clipped to his belt and a scepter of authority in his right hand.

Eventually the white plaza of Imperial Square fell away behind them; the ground made a descent and they were soon amid the squalor of the Suburro, the apartment blocks crowding out the sky, the discarded refuse laying there in the sun, the pigs, the chickens, the dogs and cats scurrying before them, the streets— packed with people—fleeing like those of an enemy tribe before Varro's might.

Onward he pressed, the scepter of authority in hand. The street made a fork, and the abandoned shell of the Tavern of the Red Lord lay before him. Varro scoured the streets, searching for any sympathizers.

The people of the Suburro were his own, but now he viewed them as the East Siders did, with scorn and derision. He wondered how many of them had committed crimes; how many of these dull-clothed, impoverished commoners had committed theft or fraud or murder and escaped the watchful eye of Lady Justice. All were suspect; all could be servants of Maria Domina, or friends of her. How many belonged to the Order of the Red Hand? How many of these impoverished scum had found solace in that cult? He would pry the truth out of them, these vagrants, these ne'er-do-wells, these people who dwelt in filth.

The Tavern of the Red Lord, a vacant building according to city records, had been operating as a registered business.

"Men of the urban cohorts." Varro wheeled around on his horse. "I give you this charge. Find me a member of the Red Hand. Bring him or her to me. You have until sundown."

The people of this filthy place called the Suburro had several market squares of their own, but one—full of trash and dung—was where most congregated. It was called Eagle Square, and in Varro's youth—though he'd never admit it—he had spent summer nights there with his friends. It had deteriorated in that time, and there were open potholes in the bricks.

In the evening light, some vendors were there, selling food and wine and various housewares. The prostitutes had recently emerged, like creatures of the night; they wore tunics over their bodies, and they called after Varro as he rode, knowing he would do nothing about them.

He rode on a white destrier, the steed of a conqueror or military official. The people here scurried before him. Even these people, the thieves and ne'er-do-wells of the Suburro, cowered before him; they knew his authority. He had been born here but he was not of here. He bore the authority of Imperium, the authority of the government.

"Secure the area!" Varro shouted, and the some dozen members of the urban cohort behind him took up their whips and began driving the people from Eagle Square. Soon it would be empty. But it would not remain that way for long; Varro was slow to anger, but it had boiled over. Tonight, after the sun set, there would be a show for the vagrants of the Suburro, a show better than any they could find at the Imperial Hippodrome or the Arena. It would be a show to spread fear in the hearts of those who defied Imperium, fear in the hearts of those who defied the Empire.

~

It was dark when the first of the urban cohorts returned to Eagle Square. It was almost pitch black, and the apartment blocks surrounding the square were lit only by candles. Amid the chirping of night birds and the rattling of distant wagons, the barking and baying of dogs, Varro looked up and saw people peeking down from windows. They thought they were safe but they were not. Who knew how many of them were in league with Maria Domina? Every member of the Red Hand was complicit in Julia's disappearance; they all shared responsibility for joining that foul cult, a cult which—as far as Varro could gather—had hidden its intentions and its beliefs from the Imperial government. But nothing should be hidden from the emperor.

One by one the urban cohorts began to trickle back to Imperial Square, most of them empty handed, but eventually some came with captives in tow. They were Suburro people if Varro had ever seen them, dressed in poor clothes, dull greys and browns. Men and women they were, young and old, and as they were dragged into their place they were defiant. One woman, old and white haired, spat at Varro as she was dragged into the center of Eagle Square.

Eventually all members of the urban cohorts were presents, hundreds in number. The captives were in the center of the square, tied in binds.

Torture was not allowed for Imperial citizens, but these were extraordinary circumstances. He would frighten them; he would make them think that was what he would do.

Out of the darkness of the streets devices of torture began to be rolled out. There were thumbscrews and racks, laughing chairs and water chambers. They were what was used on foreign enemies, and if any of these Suburro vagrants had an idea of the law they'd know they were safe.

But in the torchlight, as the urban cohorts stood among them, some had begun to back away. A woman was weeping. A man tried to run, but was slammed to the ground and pinned by one of the soldiers.

"Tell me," Varro said, "of the Red Hand. Tell me of the Tavern of the Red Lord."

Chapter Fourteen

Tidus Sulpicius Varro, Marshal of the Guard

The Red Hand, as the woman described it, believed that a new world order was possible, a world order of peace and prosperity under one they called the "Red Lord."

Who was this "Red Lord?" She could not explain; only one who had moved up the ranks of that criminal organization knew much about the true beliefs.

Varro, sitting in the palace library, was penning down all that they had learned about this monstrous cult.

The things the various captives had told him were contradictory and complicated, and their versions of what they knew didn't quite mesh.

But all agreed that the woman who called herself Maria Domina was the leader of the Red Hand in Imperial City, and one of the highest ranking members of the cult. She had vanished weeks ago.

It seemed the Red Hand attracted the lower echelons of society, those who were hopeless, who had no future. They hoped for what they called a "Red Dawn," where all would be equal, where the Empire had fallen.

And despite their treasonous beliefs, Varro—because they had told him all they knew—had let them go without further harassment.

Theirs was a twisted world, a twisted view of life, and as the morning sun peeked through the library window, Varro realized that he pitied these people, who had such an unrealistic hope.

One question remained… if the Red Hand was involved in the abduction of Julia Seánus, then why?

The Red Hand cult hated the Empire and the emperor, but

that didn't seem motivation enough to commit such a ghastly crime. And to what end was that ghastly crime committed? There was still so much for Varro to learn, so much for him to uncover. He had only begun his inquiry.

The slum people of the Suburro had given in to his threats; they had believed, erroneously, he had the powers of torture. And they had told him what they knew.

All was well, one could say. But he was no closer to finding Julia Seánus, and none, under the threat of torture, told him where Maria Domina was.

"Varro." The voice of Thedus stunned him from his work.

Varro turned to see his deputy with a letter in hand.

"This was intended for you," Thedus said.

The letter was sealed in red. He recognized instantly Maria Domina's sigil. But it would have to wait.

He took it and set it on the table. Before he ventured on in this twisted journey, he would finalize his writings for the Imperial Library. Then, posterity would know of this cult, and future emperors would not be ignorant of it.

He wrote, through the morning and in the afternoon. He wrote until his fingers ached. Maria Domina could wait.

Chapter Fifteen

Publius Allius Corvus

The mountain roads were difficult, and even now, this late in the spring, parts were clogged with snow. Where they were going, no one would tell them. Where they were going, none knew. But the one taking them there, the centurion Caro, had let slip a few times, careless words he had never elaborated upon, words he had visibly regretted. He said they were taking them to a "temple," but why an entire legion was posted at a temple was impossible to imagine.

As Publius was venturing up an especially steep road with a snow-covered valley appeared far below, and his heart raced in his chest as he saw how many fathoms it was to the bottom. Something about heights never ceased to frighten him, and he tried to gain control of himself; if he were to join the Second Anthanian with these new recruits, he'd need all the bravery he could muster, for it was the legionary's task to defend the Empire against her enemies.

Caro shouted and raised his hand. The recruits stopped behind. Rocks fell. Publius looked up into the stony mountainside ahead. A dark figure darted just out of view. He recalled the woman he had seen, the woman dressed in fine furs and rich regalia. He remembered her face, and his fear returned, fear not of death but of something else entirely, something he could not put his finger on, something he could not explain.

After a moment's halt, Caro mumbled something indistinguishable. He gave the signal and continued his march onward, up the steeping road, up the wind-blown, icy path.

They had now been in the mountains for three weeks, and each day their sojourn took them further away from civilization, further away from help.

Night settled over the mountains.

Caro gave them their ration of waybread and salted pork. Water was their drink, as it had been since they'd started. How Publius craved wine, the way it bubbled in the glass, the way it filled one's mouth with flavor. But wine was something they could not have. Only hardship was ahead. When he had left the slums of Imperial City he had expected to be taxed to the limit. And taxed to the limit he had been. There were no simple pleasures in life anymore.

The wind was blowing; the moon had arisen. The stars were twice as bright in the mountains—pinpoints of light they were, brilliant lanterns against a dark canvas. He could see on that canvas that the Dog was rising, that summer was upon them. Yet here, this high up, on the roof of the world, there was only icy wind and blowing snow. The air was not only cold but it was also thin, and though they had already settled down for the night and begun to construct their tents, Publius felt exhausted and out of breath. He did not know how he could make it another day; but he thought that every night. Every morning he woke up. Every morning he marched onward, into the afternoon, through these blasted mountains. He went to bed sure he would fail, but in the morning there was vigor, strength, and hope.

He sat by the fire, chewing at his portion of salted pork. One by one, Caro and his recruits began to retire to bed. One by one they fell asleep, until it was only Publius with his eyes open, sleeping beside the dying embers, staring out into the vast expanse, at the moon and the constellations. The wind had ceased; all had become silent.

Publius thought of home; he thought of his choice to join the legion. Doubt began to creep into his mind. Had he done the right thing? Had he?

In the mountainside up above, pebbles fell, something scurried away. It was too dark to see, too dark to make anything out. But Publius kept quiet. He would not bother his compatriots. He would not stir them from their rest.

Yet these days and weeks had convinced him of one thing: that they were not alone up here, though these roads were, according to common knowledge, utterly deserted. They were not alone, and whether spirit or mortal haunted these peaks he did not know.

He knew only that he, and these other recruits, were intruding upon something, though he did not know what, or why.

Chapter Sixteen

Tidus Sulpicius Varro, Marshal of the Guard

Varro had told no one of the letter from Maria Domina. He had learned his lesson that informing the Imperial Council meant informing the entire city. He had kept the letter secret for some time, but one morning in his private chamber, several days after he'd received it, he broke the seal and allowed it to unravel.

Varro, Varro, Marshal of the Guard.

The letters were exactly shaped, formed perfectly, set in deep dark ink. Varro wondered where Maria Domina had acquired such excellent skills at penmanship. They were the work of an educated woman, an upper class woman. What would an educated woman be doing in the Suburro, thick in the midst of this perverted cult?

It was quaint you thought you could extract the truth from the Red Hand. In the Eloesian fable of the North Wind, it is not the strong wind but the gentle sun that makes the hero take off his cloak. Why violence, Varro? It never works.

If you wish to see me, meet me at the Rock of Saturnus in two weeks' time, that is, the fourteenth of Aurelios, when the light first pierces the fog. At dawn, I shall tell you all you need to know. I will tell you where to find the one you seek.

Come alone, unarmed and unarmored. Else, you shall not hear what you need to hear. You will not find what you wish to find.

Sincerely,
Maria Domina

The Rock of Saturnus lay on the southwest edge of the peninsula, an undeveloped region by the turbid sea. It was a treacherous place for ships, difficult to navigate and a naval graveyard.

He would find this Maria Domina, in the place she sought to meet him. He would arrest her and her cretinous followers. He would mete out justice to her in Imperial Square. All this was bigger than Julia; all this was bigger than the emperor's missing daughter. He would root out the Order of the Red Hand; he would demolish it. He would pull it out by its root.

Chapter Seventeen

Publius Allius Corvus

One night, when Publius had given up all hope of reaching his destination, when he had come to believe he would be marching through these mountains until he was old and gray, he fell into a light and troubled sleep, and was almost instantly awakened.

The woman was there, walking amid the sleeping bodies, stepping over them into the newfallen snow as she made her way toward Publius.

It was the Woman of the Mountain, the one who had frightened him, the one who had terrified him. And yet as he saw her luscious lips, her bright and brilliant eyes, her blonde hair, he felt a peace come over him like he'd never felt before, a hope of good company.

Her furs were rich, of sable and ermine, white and brown and black. Her fingers were studded with rings, rings of gold and silver inlaid with emeralds and rubies and sapphires. Diamond earrings gleamed on her ears; she was a rich woman, and though she was in a fur coat she was lightly dressed. The dress she wore was thin, and her stockings were thinner. She wore not boots but sandals.

"You must be cold," Publius said. But she put a finger to his lips.

"Publius," the woman said, "you are about to enter into danger. I told you to flee. You did not listen. So do something else instead; hide a weapon in your clothing. Do not enter into the temple unarmed."

Then in a flash she was gone, as if the wind had carried her away, as if she had disappeared into the ether. In the blink of an eye she was nowhere to be found. And Publius was cold and alone, more fearful than ever of what had happened, more anxious than ever of what he faced ahead.

~

At noon the next day the road ended. Atop a high peak a metal gate had been left open; there was a windswept courtyard and a pillared temple whose roof was covered in snow. A few figures, garbed in black hoods, approached.

"Where," Publius breathed, "is the legion?"

In truth, over the past few days, he had begun to doubt everything; he had begun to think Caro had been lying the whole time. Now his thoughts were proven. It was so.

He had hidden a dagger in his tunic, and as the black garbed temple attendants made their way across the courtyard, his heart raced; but he knew he was prepared. "What is this place?" Publius said, and as he spoke the words, there were murmurs behind him, confused mutterings from the foolish recruits. They had believed Caro's lie, and so had Publius for a while.

"What is this place?" Publius said again, and this time his voice had a note of anxiety.

Caro turned around. He was wearing his helmet, and over his face there was a dark smile.

"Welcome," he said, "to the temple. You are to be initiated into the order. You are to be sacrificed to *him*."

Him. He said the word as if it were greater than a person. What god did these people worship?

"Not a god at all," one of the hooded figures said, and Publius gasped. The gate creaked shut behind them. The snow was blowing. The winds picked up. They were on the roof of the world, utterly abandoned. The knife could not protect him, not from all these people. The Woman of the Mountain had been wrong.

The men in the black hoods ushered them onward. Into the

throes of the temple they walked. The corridors were icy and bare, without ornament. Stairs took them lower and lower, into the mountain from which the temple had been carved.

Then the darkness fell away; an oculus let in sunlight from high above. They were in a spacious room, and in the center of the room was a statue of basalt, so black it seemed it was carved from shadow. It was the form of a man, and he was holding his hands together, looking down. It was as if the light was bouncing off of him. It was as if the light was rejecting him.

"What is this?" Publius cried, and a terrible panic consumed him. He had become like an animal, screaming and afraid. "What is this?" Caro grabbed his right hand, a hooded temple attendant his left. "What is this?" Publius cried again, and he twisted around, trying to free himself from his restrainers' grip.

"What is this?" he cried a third time. He did not understand his fear, his anxiety. He did not know where it welled from; he did not know from whence it came.

"Come, acolyte," the hooded man said, "to Imperial City, to see the one who will come."

Publius jerked away, freeing himself. He grabbed his dagger from his tunic. The blade gleamed in the light of the oculus.

Caro screamed, but Publius was too quick; he plunged the knife into Caro's heart. Blood began to spurt. There was a commotion underway; panic overtook the room, left and right recruits running, black hooded attendants drawing clubs. Publius turned to flee; he bolted up the stairs, sprinting as fast as he could, and the attendants could not keep up.

He fled down the temple courtyard, across the snow-swept stones. He barreled his way across the expanse; he charged straight for the gate, and so swift was he, so strong was he, that the gate burst open, and he was free.

By now a blizzard had begun to rage, and snow was falling in sheets, cloaking him in white. He began to run back down the road, the road he had come from.

He collapsed at the Woman of the Mount's feet.

"Come," she said, "with me, and we shall do the bidding of the gods."

Chapter Eighteen

Tidus Sulpicius Varro, Marshal of the Guard

Imperial City was a great sprawling behemoth, and long after you departed its pulsing urban center there were countless towns and neighborhoods clustered together. As the first sign of nature appeared, cypresses and clifftop villas, Varro uttered a prayer of thanksgiving, though to which god he did not know. Soon a cool breeze was blowing through the hills, and the tufts of golden grass were swaying. Varro had not left the city's perimeter in more than a year, but he was glad to be rid of it. He wished he were leaving it for better reasons.

But no; under cover of night he would appear at the Rock of Saturnus. Maria Domina and her despicable Red Cult would find him unawares, unarmed and prepared to sacrifice himself. But he, ten of the Imperial Guard and three urban cohorts would be waiting. They would lay hold of Maria Domina, the members of the Red Hand, and ferry them to a place where Imperial law did not hold sway. They would take her to their ally across the sea, in the City of Zoar, where torture was not prohibited. They would find uncover the network of Red Hand cultists; they would identify every last one. They would expunge it from existence.

That, at least, was the plan.

~

Westwards the road led, through the hill country, and the ground ascended as the three-thousand footsoldiers and Imperial guards marched. It would take them no less than five days to reach their destination, and even before they arrived the trap was being laid. The Empire had a policy of religious toleration, but an exception would have to be made. These people, after all, had kidnapped the emperor's daughter; what else were they capable of?

But as he walked, he knew something deeper was at bay. This mission had been his own; he had not told the emperor all he knew, that Maria claimed to know where Julia was. He only thought Varro was venturing westwards to establish order, to crush a subversive cult. Varro had read the letter and then he had tossed it into the fire.

That night, under moon and stars, he prayed to Tyrus, god of war, for success. And when he had said the words, a coldness and emptiness came over him, and he was full of fear.

Chapter Nineteen

Tidus Sulpicius Varro, Marshal of the Guard

The Rock of Saturnus appeared on the horizon. On this southwestern edge of the peninsula, a cold fog had rolled in, and it was as if he were in the throes of winter. Like a cold breath the fog was, an icy kiss on the skin. He was chilled and exhilarated, nearly frozen yet totally refreshed. This cold fog was omnipresent on the coast.

Beyond the great Rock of Saturnus, shaped like an anvil, was the sea, and the wind was churning up high waves. It was the fourteenth of Aurelios, at dawn, and the morning light was shining, and the figure of Maria Domina was there, cloaked in a red hood. She was smiling, and her eyes were haughty.

"Varro, Marshal of the Guard," she said. "You intended to slay me, to ferry me off to some desert kingdom. But know that the Red Lord has agents even in the palace."

Varro froze.

He had not expected this.

He put on an undaunted face. She had proven herself a fiercer foe, but she would not be drawn out of this alive.

"I am Maria Domina, Servant of the Red Lord," she said. "He is coming… and when a knife pierces the heart of the emperor, and the White Throne sits empty, he shall appear, and bring in the glorious dawn."

Interlude I

Across the Imperial City, in the darkness of the night, rumor spread like ravenous wildfire… the emperor had been murdered. The emperor had been murdered!

"Where was the Imperial Guard?" some asked.

Others recalled the morning when the skies were colored red, and believed all this to be a sign of coming doom, a sign of the world's end.

The Imperial Council was summoned. Furious deliberations were made. And other news reached them… news of a city on the northwest coast, of the first defeat in generations.

"The Empire will fall!" many said, some in fear and some in joy.

"The Empire will fall! It will fall!"

Chapter Twenty

Achiba

Bound and gagged, Achiba was, as soon as he reached the lower fortress. Bound and gagged, and his mother did nothing to stop them. The temple servants had seized him in the lower reaches of the city keep; with cord they had bound him and with cloth they had gagged him.

He wailed as he was jerked this way and that. He wailed as he was forced up the stone ramp. He refused to walk and they began to drag him, grinding his legs against the stone.

His mother followed and said nothing; his mother followed and did not protest. The people of the city, who had gathered underneath the keep, were leaving its safety. They were following the temple servants as Achiba was dragged up the ramp, out of the keep and into the cold night air.

~

A statue was there in the city square, a statue that had not been there before. It was made of bronze, and underneath its metal dais a fire was raging, coals and embers and scorching flame. The statue was so hot it had a note of red to its color, and its eyes, blazing, lit up the night. In Belpheor's likeness it was, a man with the head of a bull, with a single finger lifted up to the heavens.

Achiba screamed in vain.

The High Priest Drubal was there, before the statue, eyes beaming, the crystals of his fish hat twinkling in the light. He was ecstatic.

The people of the city had gathered, though the battle continued to rage, though the Imperials continued their siege.

Unprotected, the citizens of Eioli had ventured out into the open air.

The statue of Belpheor was glowing, so hot it was almost molten.

Achiba screamed again in vain, in vain.

"Awake!" Drubal was dancing. "Awake, our great lord! Awake like you once were! And we shall worship you as we did in olden times! Our sacrifices from hereon shall please you, our great and baleful lord!"

"Mother!" Achiba screamed but she had joined the jackals; she had abandoned him.

"Mother!" he screamed again, again in vain, as all his screams had been.

"Mother! Mother! Mother!"

They jerked him up a twisting staircase, and though he resisted they were too strong; up and up he clambered, against his will, against all decency. Up and up he went, forced up the winding steps, until he could feel the heat from the great statue, the great and blazing statue. From the top of the steps it was a long drop to Belpheor's molten hands, and a fiery pit below.

"Avenge me!" he said, not to his mother, not to his father, not to the people of Eioli who he now hated. "Avenge me!" he said to the wind, or to some other god, or to whoever would listen.

They pushed him off the platform, and into the fiery hands he fell, as he fused with the molten bronze and began to burn away.

Chapter Twenty-One

Drubal, High Priest of Belpheor

"Ya Belpheor! Ya Belpheor!" Drubal cried. "Ya Belpheor! Ya Belpheor!"

As the victim burned away, he could feel something change, in his heart and in the city outside of it. Darkness had long fallen over the earth, and it was night. But he felt the wind pick up, twisting this way and that.

Their god had awakened. He could feel it.

~

Sores appeared on the faces of the Imperial legionaries, great gaping red sores. There were flashes of light and bursts of thunder. The earth seemed to shake, angry at what had been done. From the battlements Drubal watched, sick with fear and overcome with fascination. He felt spirits twist about him this way and that, driving him forward and then behind. The Imperials below began to flee. Victory! Victory!

But at what cost?

Drubal had begun to feel sick.

Part Two

Chapter Twenty-Two

Publius Allius Corvus

Through the snow Publius had wandered, in a daze. Over ice-licked rocks and forgotten valleys he had made his way downwards, following the Woman on the Mount where she led him. The knife with which he had killed Caro was still fresh with blood, and his hand was trembling. He had committed the murder in a panic and now he knew whatever came after, he could never join the legion. He would be a wanted man. The legions killed you for desertion; what would they do to a recruit who slew his commander?

Yet off roads he followed the Woman on the Mount, who had claimed she would lead him to safety. She was all he had now; she was the only one left who would speak to him.

The further down he climbed, the more treacherous the journey seemed to become. Frequently he would slip on rocks and tumble an inch down the slopes. Snow was continuing to fall, less than before but still in substantial flakes. The wind was biting and icy, and it was difficult to breathe in the thin mountain air.

By the time he reached the base of the valley he was stumbling, with little balance to his steps. The snow had picked up again; the woman he was following had slowed her gait. She was only a faint silhouette. "Hurry!" she said. "Follow me!" They ran and ran as the winds howled and the snow fell in sheets. They ran until they were both panting. And then, suddenly, they were in the heart of a cave, far removed from the elements. The darkness was total, but the figure of the Woman on the Mount—oddly enough— seemed to glow. There was faint illumination.

Publius wondered if she was a spirit of some kind, and not a woman. She was not dressed for the elements; she was dressed as a rich woman walking through the streets of Imperial City. Her fur coat looked more for ornament than for warmth. The leggings she wore were thin, with little more consistency than silk.

But even in this cave, Publius feared he would freeze. Night was here, and each moment the temperature dropped further. When he breathed, he breathed in fog. He was ill prepared, ill equipped, and with only this woman to keep him company.

Yet despite his shivering, despite his discomfort, when he looked upon the woman before him, all he could think about was questions. What was a woman of such beauty and refinement doing here, so far from civilization? Why was she not shivering? Why did her body give off light?

"Who are you?" Publius said through chattering teeth.

"Hush, hush," she said, "and I will tell you everything. Here… one moment."

Seemingly from thin air she drew a glass lantern, and it emitted light. Far in the corner of the cave, there was a tattered cot, a chest, and scattered bits of clothing.

"An adventurer once took shelter here," she said. "It should keep you warm for the night. But you are not safe here. The Temple Watchers will be after you."

The Temple Watchers. There were times for questions, and now was not such a time.

"What about you? Will you stay warm?" Publius said.

"I am not here," the woman answered, "not in the way you think I am."

"What do you mean?" Publius said.

"You are only seeing me," the woman said. "I am Julia, the emperor's daughter, and though I speak to you where you are, I am half a world away."

Chapter Twenty-Three

Tidus Sulpicius Varro, Marshal of the Guard

The past week had been a blur to him.

The escape of Maria Domina was something he had largely let happen.

But returning home to the city, to see that her devious plans had all succeeded, that the Imperial Palace—having lost some of its protection—was an easy target...

The emperor had been murdered in his sleep. The assassins had been spotted, and the tabards they wore were marked with a red hand.

Varro sat in his room, staring blankly over the balcony, wondering what would happen to him. Would he be stripped of his post? The Imperial Council was convening now. He knew that the nation was in a crisis, that Varro's honor and employment was the least of their concerns. But staring out the balcony, at the Empire's capital, he could not help but wonder, and worry.

Varro had never been prone to feeling, but he felt guilty in a way he never had before. He felt as if he at least in part had caused this. That Maria Domina had outsmarted him was beyond question. And he had let her slip from his fingers.

Dark days were ahead for the Empire, dark days. And he wondered if it could weather the storm. The conquest of the peninsula had taken decades, and there were times after the Unification that it seemed the Empire might fall. But now was a precarious moment, and in the tensions of the city's ethnic discord, he wondered if the death of the emperor might cause things to finally spiral out of control. As the chief commander of the urban cohorts, he had taken great pains to establish order, and now it seemed that a stray spark, a small gout of flame, might incite the city into pandemonium.

There was a knock on the door.

Varro turned, left the balcony. "Who is it?" he shouted.

He opened the door to see a woman he'd never seen before. She was dark, with thick black hair, and there were two diamond rings on her ears. She had the look of an easterner. Her robe was scarlet with green trimmings. Over her there hung a scent of perfume, a powerful perfume with a note of pine.

"Are you Tidus?" she said. "Tidus Sulpicius Varro?"

No one called him that. She clearly had seen his name in some registry.

"My name is Isadora," she said. "I am from the city of Pelagios."

Varro had not heard of such a city.

"I… I was wondering… if we could speak in private."

~

At the bottom level of the Imperial Palace, in a space open to the sun, were the gardens where a variety of plants grew. Fig trees were there in abundance, and the emperor—gods rest his soul—could often be seen picking the fruit from them when harvest time came. In addition to figs there were plants of varying utility, moonfruit and starfruit, veritable forests of basil, flowers of all kinds, and enough fountains to care for all the palace residents. There were benches aplenty, places to sit, and to a quiet corner Varro led this "Isadora." He had nothing better to do, and anything to take his mind off his failures was welcome.

Isadora sat across from him on another bench.

"What is it?" Varro said.

"I came from across the sea, Caius Sulpicius Varro. I came to you because I had a dream," Isadora said.

"You came all this way because you had a dream?" Varro

repeated demurely. "And you were let in? I am the master of the Imperial Guard. Another failure on my part…"

"You could say I am on official business," Isadora said. "The city of Pelagios is known for its perfumes. I had hoped to open up trade with the Empire."

Perfumes. That explained much. But the Empire had become too soft and luxurious already. They were losing their old values, the values of the simple life, of the farm, the home and hearth and when required the sword.

"Perfumes," Varro repeated.

"Yes," she said. "That is why the archon sent me here. But I had another reason. I saw you, Caius Sulpicius Varro… I saw you, and I saw a star trampled on the ground, a star fastened to a golden chain, lying unattended on the ground."

Varro gulped. He tried not to hide his shock. What had been the heirloom he found? The "star," the glowing gem that the emperor's daughter Julia had worn around her neck?

"A star," Varro continued. "On the ground? What do you mean?"

"A star trampled on the ground," Isidora said. "An army bearing red standards. A man marching before the army, girt in crimson armor. Then there was war, and the end of all things. I saw a name… Nivus… and heard a voice say yours—'Caius Sulpicius Varro.'"

Varro did not know what to tell this woman, if he should tell her anything or just let her be on her way. "A star," she said.

"Find the star, Varro," Isidora continued. "That is what the dream told me. That was what was whispered to me. Find the star, Varro, and you shall find answers."

But what had been done with the star? And what was its purpose?

Varro supposed he would soon find out.

Chapter Twenty-Four

Publius Allius Corvus

Publius, wrapping himself in the cot as if it were a blanket, still could not shake the icy cold or the thin mountain air. Julia had sat down beside him, but she was incorporeal, and if he tried to touch her hand, his would go straight through.

She had told him wild stories… of a power she had discovered early in her youth, of a propensity she did not fully understand which her father had tried to accept but never quite come around to.

"I have walked these mountains many times." Julia was looking straight at him. "In this state, I have. I know these paths.

"In my youth, in the palace, I would oft fall asleep. I would think on other parts of the world; I would travel by sky or by sea. Every night, in my dreams, I would visit other places. My father did not believe my stories until I began to appear to him."

"The palace," Publius repeated. "You are Julia Seánus… The emperor's daughter."

In his life in the Imperial slums, Publius had heard talk of Julia, the emperor's radiantly beautiful daughter. He had heard legionaries make dirty jests of her. She was considered a style setter in Imperial City, and the women there would copy her clothing and her hairstyle.

But when Publius first saw her, he never would have guessed it was her, that the emperor's own daughter was appearing before him.

"I am the emperor's daughter," Julia said. Her incorporeal body seemed to waver. No, it was her eyes that were watering. "But he is dead, I have learned. He is dead, Publius. He has gone on to the next world."

The next world. Julia was so devout that the people of Imperial City knew it, and on every high holy day she could be found attending temple. That was what his fellow citizens told him.

"I fear the Empire is headed toward troubled times," Julia said.

"I can handle troubled times," Publius said.

"That is what many say about troubled times, and yet, when they fall on them, they haven't the strength." Julia stood up. "As soon as the storm breaks, we should get to lower ground. There are monsters in these mountains, not just the Temple Watchers."

That was another thing that had been bothering Publius. "The temple… the statue… what was it?"

"A thing so terrible you will not want to know of," Julia said, "for when the horror of it dawns on you, you will be assailed… appalled."

Publius would take Julia's word for it.

"The Empire is destined for greatness," Julia said. "But it is better to live in a good nation than a great one. Greatness is a burden, and with it comes strife and punishment."

Publius' mind returned to the statue, which seemed to shun all light, totally black in color… a man staring at his hands.

Outside the wind was howling. There was a distant cry, barely audible, a cry like the shout of a man, but more strained, more hoarse.

"What was that?" Publius said.

"What did you hear?" Julia said. "In this state I can only see… I can only hear the voice of the one I've projected to."

"A loud cry," Publius said. "Like a man, but…."

"The Men of the Mountain roam here," Julia said. "That is what I call them. Furry beasts, offspring of the Blighted Temple. If you venture out into the snow, they will find you. Stay still, Publius. Ready your sword."

Publius drew his sword out an inch from the hilt. The metal

gleamed.

There was another cry, but it was more distant, more disoriented.

"The winds will hide your scent if you remain calm," Julia said. "Many cannot remain calm in their presence. But I have a feeling you can."

Publius waited. The winds howled; the snow picked up pace and then began to dwindle. Downward, downward, the white flakes fell, like feathers drifting through air. Publius breathed deeply. There was another cry, more distant than the second one. The Men of the Mountain were moving away from him. They were leaving him alone.

Quietly, Publius began to speak once more. "Julia… you say you are projecting yourself. You say you are appearing from afar. Where are you?"

"I will lead you to me," Julia said, "but first, there is something for you to accomplish. Something only you can do."

Chapter Twenty-Five

Publius Allius Corvus

"You want me to do something?" Publius said.

He wondered if he had it in him. He, after all, was a wanted man now. Deserters from the Imperial Army were killed; what, therefore, was the punishment for murdering your superior? Caro the centurion was dead at his hand. He had disobeyed his orders. He had murdered a man in cold blood and then fled the scene of the crime. If he wanted to live he would take up with brigands. He could never show his face in Imperial City again.

"I want you to go to a place called the Rock of Saturnus," Julia said. "There you will utter these words: 'The Red Lord cometh.' Then your task will be done."

"The Red Lord cometh?" Publius repeated the words. Perhaps, Julia was not the wise, devoted public figure everyone knew her as. Perhaps, there was a trace of madness in the Seánus family line, one that skipped every few generations but found its way into one of its most beautiful members. Family trees are twisted things, and there is always a chance of a bad branch.

But no. He peered into Julia's eyes, those brilliant blue orbs, and saw nothing except a warm spirit, one full of love but also of wisdom.

The winds outside had ceased; light was peeking through the clouds.

"Get up," Julia said, "and follow me."

Chapter Twenty-Six

Agatho Lornodoris, Speaker of the Council

The Council had assembled, Augusts all, representing the thirty wards of Imperial City. The marble of the Council Hall was white, and its red seats circled the space between.

"*Numera!*" Lornodoris cried and at once the Legis began to count those assembled there.

"One, two, three," the Legis began, and ended at twenty-seven.

A quorum was present, enough for the assembly to be legally convened. The business of the nation could be conducted now. Laws could be passed; and Agatho, together with his fellow Councilors, could attempt to halt the downward spiral the Empire had found itself in.

"Friends, fellow Councilors, Augusts all," Lornodoris said, "the White Throne sits empty, and as such the Council by vote has established its emergency powers. Until a new emperor is named, it is our task to halt this crisis we have found ourselves in."

"Objection!" cried Councilor Constantius, who represented Kings Terrace.

But the Legis strode forth before the assembled seats. "Out of order… Let the Speaker finish."

"Friends, fellow Councilors, Augusts all," Lornodoris said again, this time with a sneer on his face. Constantius was always a thorn in his side, whenever he entered the Council House—a friend outside, a pathological enemy within.

"The White Throne is empty, and as such the Council has its emergency powers," Lornodoris went on. "Until a new emperor is named, we must govern the country. I propose we vote to give this body the full powers of government, by majority vote, until this crisis is resolved, until Imperium shows its will."

Imperium, the god of the Empire, was a human invention; he according to his priests represented the will of the people and was not numbered among the heavenly host. In the end, it would have to be the Imperial Council who named the emperor, by a two-thirds vote, but thus far no man in the palace had been proven capable or deserving of trust.

"Objection!" Councilor Constantius said, and the Legis raised his hand.

"Granted," the Legis said. "The Councilor from Kings Terrace may speak."

The Legis retreated to the edge of the chamber and Constantius climbed down from his seat, striding before the light of the great central oculus.

Lornodoris in turn drew backward; the Speaker of the Council was never forced to sit. He could watch from the perimeter. He was the chief among them, vested with certain powers and privileges, but also great responsibilities.

Constantius glared at Lornodoris, then turned to regard the other twenty-eight Councilors haughtily. They were all old, gray or white haired, and their tunics were the color of snow, accented with purple sashes.

"A nation cannot be ruled by thirty," Constantius said. "We are engaged in a war with the Ugars, a war we are inexplicably losing. The cities are beginning to break free, even those who called themselves 'Friends of the Empire.' The next time you are in Imperial City's streets, look into the eyes of a child and ask, do they deserve to be ruled by thirty men who cannot agree on anything? Do they deserve to be ruled by thirty doddering fools?"

"Objection!" Lornodoris said. "Insulting a member of the body."

"Do not explain." The Legis strode forth; Constantius retreated. "Nonetheless, I rule you correct. Constantius, return; you have broken the rule. You may speak no more during this session of Council."

Constantius grumbled, though he surely knew what he was doing. He knew the laws and rules, the precedents that had been set, the rituals and processes that had developed over the Council's hundreds of years of existence. The Imperial Council dated to before the Unification; the Council was present when the Empire was ruled by kings. Of its rules and precedents there was no end to learning; only the Legis came close to mastery.

One of the Councilors left his seat. It was Valerius, the Councilor from Mud Bottom. He was the youngest of them, with equal gray to his black hair, with steely, hawkish eyes and Imperial aquiline nose. In matters of war he always delighted; in matters of war he was the first to call for troops, the first to demand the blood of young Imperials, and the most vicious to the Empire's enemies.

"My Signore Speaker," Valerius said, "I ask for the floor."

"I consent," the Speaker said.

"Overruled." The Legis raised his hand. "The Oculus passes noon. The Council shall not meet until dusk."

Only then did Lornodoris notice the sun shining in the floor's exact middle. He wondered what the cause was of such a rule, a rule that severely limited the business of government. Perhaps, the ancient Imperials, living in the Peregothian Isles, were more directly affected. The Council did not always have a Council House; in its early days it met outside. Braving the elements was a sign of its dedication, and its commitment to the Imperial People.

"I consent to the Legis' instruction," Lornodoris said.

By a two-thirds vote, he could keep the Council in session. But he had a feeling about today. And as the session began, he had begun to think of the implications of his grand proposal. A takeover of government by the Imperial Council was a sign of true crisis. He needed a little more time to think things over, a little more time to plot, to strategize. The burden of it had begun to weigh on him; and he thought of the reports of the Ugars… of an entire Imperial legion fleeing from the city of Eioli. How was it possible?

"Let us say the invocation," the Legis said.

They offered up prayers to heaven, and promised to do the will of the people. They promised to convene at the setting of the sun.

~

The Council House was connected to the Imperial Palace by a great sky bridge. Which edifice was more beautiful was a hot debate among the Imperial nobility; the Council House with its mounting levels and its snow-white dome, or the Imperial Palace, a great sprawling patchwork maze of colonnades and plazas.

Lornodoris walked to the edge of the sky bridge and looked down on the city below. Each year Imperial City seemed to grow. Those homes and shops, white with red tile, were home to some two hundred thousand souls. She was one of the world's largest cities, surpassed only by the Eastern Kingdoms across the sea. Lornodoris had not always lived here; his family hailed from the Peregothian Isles, and he himself had grown up in the country northwest of here, his father serving as prelate.

Yet though it had not begun that way, it had become home to him. Imperial City was his, and he was hers. He reveled in her embrace, and she had changed him. He had begun his life as a rustic from the village of Caudera; now he was a man of the City, an Imperial Councilor with all the privileges that provided, the Speaker of the Council no less.

And yet, in all his years, in all his time keeping the peace, he had never been present at a moment like this. The spring and summer had fallen upon them; the skies had been as blood in

Imperial Harbor. The same night, the emperor's daughter had been kidnapped under the noses of the Imperial Guard. An now, the emperor himself had been slain. He was dead now, cremated and sealed in a silver jar, stored with his fellow office holders in the Temple of Imperium. He was gone, leaving the Empire rudderless.

He felt a presence behind him. "The Ugars… the Ugars! What happened?"

A hand touched his shoulder; he recognized the perfume as belonging to Signor Valerius.

The Councilor from the Suburro had exited the Council chambers. Like Lornodoris, he had decided not to return home.

"Do you remember, Valerius, when the war began?" Lornodoris said. "When we expected to crush Eioli in a matter of weeks and make an example of them to other cities? First they held out a month, then two months, then three. And now a full Imperial legion had descended into chaos; a full legion had been driven away."

"Yes, I remember," Valerius said. "I remember everything. Have you read the legate's report?"

"No," Lornodoris said. "No, I have not."

It was something he was loath to admit. It was the first great defeat in many decades; yet he had wanted to hold on to his national pride. He did not want to read the account of Imperial legionaries fleeing. He had not wanted to expose himself.

"The physicians have been treating the wounded," Valerius said. "Coin-sized sores have opened up on their skin. They are dying one by one. Do you believe in magic, Signor Speaker?"

"Magic?" Lornodoris said. "It depends on how you describe the phrase."

The powers of the augurs and the flamens were beyond dispute; no one would argue against that, though such sorcery was rarely displayed and not usually in public view.

"Magic," Valerius said, "like that that comes from gods.

"Do you know, Signor Speaker, the rituals of the old Ugars? How they would sacrifice their own children? How they would congregate on high hills to prostitute themselves? Have you heard of Belpheor? Of Daghan? Of Amman?"

When the Empire found a new enemy, slander was common. No one would sacrifice their own child. No one would prostitute themselves in the name of a god. It was against human nature. The Ugars were foreign, but they were human.

"No," Lornodoris said. "No, if that is what you mean by 'magic,' then consider me a firm skeptic."

"Then how did the legion become infected? Why were they driven away in a panic, as they describe, by 'elemental spirits?' That is the word they used," Valerius said.

"People are often mistaken," Lornodoris said. "And bad air and foul winds can create terrible sicknesses. There is a lot of sickness in this world, Valerius. There are many plagues of many kinds. The Ugars are not known for their sanitary practices.

"The gods do not intervene in the affairs of men. The heavenly host does not think of mankind. Who are we, so arrogant to think they care for the affairs of mortals, when they sit enthroned?"

Lornodoris turned to face his friend. He was the youngest of the Council at age fifty-five. He represented the most scoffed-at ward of Imperial City, home to its poor and its refuse. He was the Councilor from the Suburro of all places, and yet he was the man whom Lornodoris respected the most. He had earned Lornodoris' respect, though his ostentatious patriotism was trite at times.

"I believe the gods do intervene," Valerius said. "The gods of the heavens, and also those below. Think of it, friend. The Ugars are primitive. Their weaponry is basic… it is poorly made. The lowest legionary is better armed than the best of them.

"And yet not only did they last, month after month, now they have defeated a legion. An entire legion, friend!"

It was strange, to be sure. The Fourth Peregothian was the newest of the legions, one that had been first conscripted some five years ago. As the army expanded, new recruits were used to fill the holes. The Fourth Peregothian was the least tried, but every legion, every single one of them, was properly equipped. Every one of them was properly trained.

"We will find a rational explanation," Lornodoris said. "Shall we make a bet?"

"I suppose so," Valerius said.

"If there is no true explanation, only a supernatural one, then I shall retire my position as Speaker of the Council and appoint you in my place," Lornodoris said.

"And if there is a rational explanation?" Valerius said.

"Then," Lornodoris demurred, "why, I will have your vote in all my propositions, from now until the time I die."

"So be it," Valerius said. "The deal is made."

Chapter Twenty-Seven

Publius Allius Corvus

The sun was setting when Publius reached the lowlands. A gentle breeze was blowing, buffeting him ever so much. In the trees cicadas were singing. Golden hills stretched into the interminable distance. They were not far from the shore, and the scent of saltwater was in the wind, faint and teasing.

Julia was a distant form; she had been leading him, whenever she could, out of distant mountain passes and through descending roads.

He was out of the mountains, but he felt more in danger than ever; he could scarcely breathe, and the memory of what he had done, combined with the potential consequences, never failed to frighten him. Julia was his only consolation. Julia was a light in his darkness.

And as he gotten to know her, he had begun to think things about her he was sure she did not return. Her distant form was like a dancing shadow. She had paused under the shade of a holm oak. The noises of summer were all about them, and though night was at hand, it was so hot the air was wavering. Publius was thirsty; his waterskin was dry, and he had not drunk in more than an hour.

He raced over to Julia.

Julia met him in an embrace; her incorporeal hands passed straight through him.

Julia promised she would lead him to this "Rock of Saturnus," but she had warned that her perception—in projected state—was limited, that the only person she could truly observe was Publius, that she had grafted herself, mentally, onto him. All else she could see was like peering through a foggy glass. That was how she described it. But she nonetheless knew the way; she had led him down precarious roads, down switchbacks and through hidden valleys. Publius trusted her.

"Julia," Publius said. There was shade under the holm oak, but he could not make out any water. "I need to rest."

Julia nodded. Her brilliant eyes twinkled, and she smiled. "And I must go, Publius. They might hear me talking."

"They"—Julia insisted she was not dead, that she was projecting herself from afar, that she had been imprisoned herself. At times, when she spoke to Publius, she became distracted, worried her captors would overhear. But she had never told Julia the manner of her capture or who had done the capturing.

Under this holm oak he would rest. As Julia wavered and then seemingly blinked out of existence, Publius sat down, resting his back against the tree trunk.

Memories swirled through his mind. He remembered what he had done. He had murdered a centurion, his superior. Sooner or later, he would be hunted.

A horn blew, far in the distance.

Chapter Twenty-Eight

Agatho Lornodoris, Speaker of the Council

The sun had set; the lights of the city below the sky bridge formed a dull glow, a mélange of beacon-like illumination stretching to the harbor. The air had cooled. The Council was in session once more.

When he entered the Council House's main chamber, there were fewer councilors than before. Councilor Constantius, his implacable enemy, was not present, nor was the councilor from West Village or Outer Creek.

The Legis was there, surely resentful that Lornodoris had called a nighttime meeting. It was difficult for everyone, but the nation was in crisis, and if someone did not seize the reins, all would fall apart.

"*Numera!*" Lornodoris cried, and he wondered if enough councilors would be present to convene.

Yet the Legis began counting, and ended at twenty-three. There were enough councilors willing to do their duty, enough people willing to embark on this task.

"Fellow councilors!"

In the seats, Valerius stood, eyes twinkling darkly.

"We convene at night! Nix is the goddess of night, and I move that we convene this council, on the first of Odens, in her honor," Lornodoris said.

He stood there for what seemed like several minutes. The Legis strode forward.

"No objection," the Legis said. "The Council meeting of the first of Odens, of the 210th year of the Empire, is named in honor of the goddess."

"And in the name of that goddess," Lornodoris said, "she of mysteries, she of the Silvered Stair, I move that we climb a stair of our own, a stair that will lead us out of this present calamity. The Empire requires strong leadership. We are capable of giving it. The Council has ruled before, in the absence of an emperor.

"Join me, my fellow councilors, without objection. I move we grant the office of emperor for a time of one month, to the Imperial Council. Our ancestors vested great power in this body. They believed in it; and so must we."

Perhaps it was the darkness of the night; perhaps it was the exhaustion. But the ploy worked. Lornodoris waited, second after second, moment after moment, and no councilor stirred, no councilor raised their hand.

Lornodoris backed up, yielding the floor, and the Legis strode forward in answer.

"No objection is made," the Legis said. "By default, the proposal stands. Let it be codified into law; until a month from now, the tenth of Sextil, the Imperial Council—by majority vote— assumes the powers of the White Throne."

Lornodoris smiled. For too long the authorities of the emperor had grown. The Council had made the office indispensable. The Council could make it dispensable once more.

Chapter Twenty-Nine

Publius Allius Corvus

The sound of the horns were getting closer. Every few minutes, it seemed, a loud peal echoed through the night.

It was a little cooler now, but still uncomfortably warm. Publius, in a thick tunic and long leggings, felt overdressed.

He had drawn his sword, but if it was a hunting party he knew he—a single man—could not overcome them.

But he reminded himself that news traveled slowly, that whatever occurred at that Blighted Temple would take time to reach the authorities. His crimes could not be known, not yet.

Publius stood up, sword in hand. The night was deep and dark; crickets were chirping. He backed away, retreating through the grass. He caught a trace of color; he hid behind a tree, praying to any god who would hear him that he would remain undetected.

The horn blew again, deafening in tone. There was the sound of galloping hooves, of horses' feet grinding against the grass. Soon they flew by a squadron of equites, soldiers fully armored with shining silvery breastplates. Their horses were armored too. On their helmets were the red plumes of the Imperial military.

Publius thought he had removed every sign of his former military service, but his close cropped hair was a big clue. Instead, he ducked away and thanked the gods for the darkness that cloaked him.

This area, south of the Goldenhorn Mountains, was a prime training ground for the Army. He could not fully escape such patrols.

The summer resort of the rich, Paradise Gardens, was somewhere nearby, south of the mountains, in the foothills where a gentle breeze was more common than not. How Publius had envied those people, those people born into rich families, the Seáni, the Lornodorises, the Metellii, and others. If they joined the army they were given rich posts, ones where work and danger was far away, yet having the prestige and honors that came along with military services. They were the masters of horse, the grand legates, the strategists and tribunes. Publius had joined the army as a grunt, hoping against hope to work his way up the ranks. Ending his career as a centurion would have been within reach, but not much better.

Yet all that was past. Once he was identified, Publius Allius Corvus would be hunted like a wild deer. He could never join the army again; he could never show his face in civil society.

The equites numbered some hundred, and they were galloping by quickly. The ones toward the back of the formation were bearing torches in their hands.

The equites were a step above legionaries. By law, they had to be of the Knightly class or higher. Of all the grunt work in the army, it was the highest esteemed; but it could only be achieved by blood, not by merit. Publius uttered a faint curse at them as they rode by, but the night was too deep and dark for them to see him, and the noises of summer were too loud for them to hear. He was, as he had been when he joined the army, invisible, unexceptional, easy to miss, easy to ignore.

He had to get out of this area, where camps and battalions of soldiers were omnipresent. This was the center of the Imperial Army, where the forces of the Empire marshaled and gathered for war. It was the military's playground.

The night was deep and dark. Under the shade of the holm oak he knelt; he prayed the darkness would end. He prayed to any god who would hear him, and to every god, that Julia would show her face soon.

Chapter Thirty

Agatho Lornodoris, Speaker of the Council

In the time since the proclamation was made, Lornodoris made a point to avoid the Imperial Palace. The news that the Imperial Council had assumed, even temporarily, the powers of the White Throne was sure to inflame the coterie who thrived on the attention and the authority of the emperor. By that proclamation, not objected to by a single councilor, they had diminished the whole of the Imperial Palace and those who lived there.

Lornodoris was on the sky bridge. His work was done for the day. To get down to the streets below was easier if he ventured through the Imperial Palace, but that seemed out of bounds now. A more difficult route would have to be taken. His home in Kings Terrace awaited.

The afternoon sun was warm. Summer was at its height. Normally, at this time, councilors would speak of retiring to Paradise Gardens. But that seemed inappropriate now. Though the heat had become unbearable, it no longer seemed appropriate to retreat from Imperial City. To retreat from the city was to abandon a city and a nation in crisis. The emperor had been murdered, not long after his daughter had been kidnapped.

And who had done it? The assassins had been caught; but they had refused to speak, and their date of execution had been set. Imperial citizens had done this, stakeholders in the nation. How could it be?

~

Lornodoris, seventy years old, had outlived most of his childhood friends. His bones were weak, his joints painfully sore, but he always refused help. He made his way down through the Council House's endless staircases, down its innumerable levels. There were guards posted almost everywhere, searching for intruders, but he did not ask for their support. He wanted to consider himself capable.

When he reached the bottom, he breathed a sigh of relief. The great circular space was lit with torches, and between each torch was a statue, featuring heroes or notable men from every Imperial City Ward. It was called the Council Crypt, and it was rung with columns and banisters. It was intended to be the burial place of Anthans, the founder of Imperial City, but his family had resisted, and so the "tomb" set aside for him lay empty, without coffin or urn.

These halls were complex, with history behind each door, and in every hallway some secret had been told. In every hallway there had been a whisper, from councilor or guard. The great men of the Empire had walked through the Council House, the famed heroes of old. Lornodoris was one of them, a blueblood, a leader of the people. Emperors and great men were his friends; and in council sessions he met foreign kings and padishas. He had lived a rich life, and at seventy he hadn't a moment to reflect on it; he was as active as he had been in his youth. In fact he had more worries, now; the weight of the nation was resting on him.

He knew his way through the crypt. He walked up to the statue of Hortatus, a military hero from Canal District. Behind it, he fumbled with his hands, finding a stone that felt out of place. He pushed the stone; the masonry door opened. Into the tunnels he went, the tunnels that would take him underneath the city streets and directly home. There he would avoid the crime and thievery that dominated Imperial City at night. These tunnels had been built at the same time as the Council House. Once they had seemed unnecessary, but with the city's growth no councilor could now do without them. For councilors oft made grand promises, and were unable to fulfill them; and moreover there were dangerous cults and gangs of criminals that roamed the streets. Without an army of guards, no councilor could walk the streets safely,

In the tunnels, Agatho walked, descending into the depths of the city's subterrain. It was cool, and moist, and water was dripping from the stones. It was dark, almost pitch black, but at long intervals there were torches flaring, and lamps that gave a little light. These tunnels connected to Kings Terrace, the city's richest district, where it was assumed every councilor would reside. But some councilors came from humble origins, and it took them a while before they could afford a home on Laurel Street or Princes' Way. As for Agatho, his Kings Terrace manor—called Heron House—had been in the family since not long after the conquest of the peninsula. It was owned, wholly, by all the Laconus Lornodorises, but Agatho as the oldest of the clan was considered the manager.

He knew also of the cult activities that took place in these tunnels, old cults that were present at the time of the founding. Agatho Lornodoris had not participated in them, nor did he know all that much about the Blighted One or what they truly worshiped. But such cults were old, and many of the August class participated. Lornodoris was not one of them.

Guards were walking to and fro; far in the distance, he caught sight of Caius, the councilor from River Ford. He recalled the nights when the cult met, wearing iron masks on their faces, speaking in a language that no one could understand—a language that, according to legend, the Imperials spoke in the time before the Unification. Wearing the masks, the participants of the Blighted One cult were impossible to identify.

~

The arduous walk eventually ended, though it always

seemed it never would. Up a set of stone stairs he walked, up a trap door, and into the wine cellar of his home, where rack after rack of bottles were stored, northern whites, Anthanian reds, and the most sought after wine of all—Korthian wine, imported from the Eastern Kingdoms. It had been a stressful day, a day full of worry and care, but he knew his work was not done. The work of a councilor was never done, especially now, now that they had assumed the powers of the White Throne and were sure to garner resistance from the palace. So much needed to be done, so much time to prepare for the battle of law and afterwards, the struggle to unite the country.

He exited the wine cellar and found himself in the main hall, where portraits hung of Lornodorises past, and a great crystal chandelier dangled, and embers were burning in the hearth… and there, standing on the Fharese carpet, was one he recognized, a man who had not dared show his face in weeks.

It was Varro, the Marshal of the Guard.

He was standing there in armor, a red half cape over his shoulder.

At least he had the presence of mind to have his sword buckled in its sheath and not in hand.

Varro was staring at him.

"Do you know the punishments for intruding upon a councilor's home?" Lornodoris said.

And then it struck him, and his heart fluttered in fear; the emperor had been murdered. Was it inconceivable that the Marshal of the Guard, the one charged with his protection, had something to do with his death?

But on Varro's face a faint smile had formed.

Lornodoris had not often seen that harsh, stoic man of the military smile.

"The Council assumes the power of the White Throne," Varro said, "and the Marshal of the Guard is therefore charged with protecting it."

Chapter Thirty-One

Tidus Sulpicius Varro, Marshal of the Guard

Varro did not like the act of power-grabbing the Council engaged in. It flew in the face of custom; it showed disregard for the institutions and traditions that bound the nation together.

A faint smile had formed on Lornodoris' face.

He was an August, and not only an August but the most blue blooded of the blue bloods. His family had been in the annals of Imperial history since the founding. The Lornodorises were widely known, synonymous with wealth and privilege.

"The Marshal of the Guard," Lornodoris said, "charged with protecting the White Throne. I suppose I will not call the urban cohorts on you. But I do not require guarding."

What other laws would the Council disregard in their quest for power? A member of the Imperial Guard had been posted in every councilor's home; Varro, as the marshal, would protect the Speaker.

Would Varro allow him to further disregard laws and regulations? Having usurped the power of the emperor, would Lornodoris also defy tradition?

Yet Varro himself had ulterior motives.

He had assigned guards to the councilors this morning, when they'd just heard of the Council's plans.

He had begun to inquire lightly of where he might find Seladora's Star. He had learned the emperor was not buried with it, and so—that pendant, bound in gold chain, which had been stomped upon by Julia's captors—was in someone else's possession. But who possessed the Seánus family heirloom? It was anyone's guess. He had searched halfheartedly through Lornodoris' home but had found nothing.

What was the purpose of the Star of Seladora? In truth, the dream of that Eastern envoy had played only a small part. He recalled finding the star, which had been worn around Julia's neck, and seeing its warm glow. He wondered if there was power to it, if there was, dare he say it, magic. But wherever it was, it was not in Lornodoris' home. It was not, in his estimation, in Heron House. But it was somewhere to be found; of that he was sure.

Chapter Thirty-Two

Publius Allius Corvus

The morning light was filtering through the leaves. The cold of the night had not quite evaporated; dew was on the yellow grass, and as Publius stirred awake he felt more refreshed than he had in a long time, positively exuberant.

Ah, yes, he had forgotten his situation. He had stabbed a centurion straight through the heart, and then fled from the site of his crime.

And Julia… where on earth was Julia? Where could she be?

Normally, when he arose, she would be there with him. In fact, he could not recall a morning since the night of the crime when Julia had not been there, appearing before him.

Panic seized him. He could not face these trials alone, not without Julia his guide, his comfort.

Where could she be?

He scanned the golden hills, crowned with holm oaks. The sun was blazing and the skies were cloudless, but there was no trace of her in the heavens. Where was Julia? In these dark times, when his future plans and dreams had been shattered, she had been there, guiding him, comforting him, pushing him onward when he didn't want to take another step.

She had told him of her capture; he wondered if her captors had finally followed through on their threats, if they had killed her once and for all.

But nonetheless Publius rose; he was perfectly aware of the danger he was in.

This was northeastern Anthania, the part of the peninsula where the military predominated. Imperial citizens largely had rights; but for a soldier like him, who had taken the oath, punishments for crimes were severe. It seemed unlikely that word had spread from so far away, but he had to be on his guard, and moving through the area as a civilian would draw suspicion.

He got up, hoping and praying that Julia would find him, hoping and praying that Julia was alive and well, that he would not miss the guidance from her that he so relied upon.

He got up, hoping and praying, and he left quickly, hurrying through the hills, desperate not to be found.

~

He rounded the crest of the hill. In the distance, he caught sight of red-gold standards. A battalion of imperial troops was no doubt being trained; all these young men, from every corner of the peninsula, from the Isles and from the Empire's overseas holdings, had converged on this spot. They had left on promises of seeing the world; and like Publius many who embarked on that journey would become disappointed, disillusioned.

Publius took a turn south, huddling down as he walked, venturing between hills, as the cool of the morning evaporated and the heat of the midsummer sun began to gather.

He still had on his leather jerkin, and his sword was of finely worked steel, a standard Imperial issue. He thought of discarding them, of hiding the fact he was a soldier, but then he would be without protection in this wild world, without a way to defend himself. And so he pressed on.

~

It was the afternoon and the sun was blazing down.

Publius thought he saw long shadows in the grass, dark inky black spots that stretched from the trees. He felt faint, and though he knew he was in danger there was nothing he wanted more than to stop for the day, to put all this behind him.

"Julia," he found himself muttering. "Julia... where are you? Come back to me!"

The wind at his back was like a cold breath. He tasted something sweet in the air and his tongue tingled like he had bitten into an icicle.

He turned around and staggered backward.

Julia was there, but she was different.

He fur coat was gone; she was wearing a brown smock. The cloth was torn in parts, revealing open wounds. There was pain in her eyes, pain like he had never seen before in her.

Yet her lips were red, and her blue eyes had the warm goodness Publius had always known, though they were now watering with tears.

"Publius," she said, "I fear my time is short. They have beaten me because I refuse to tell them—to tell them—"

"To tell them what?" Publius said.

"To tell them—to tell them—?"

Her eyes seemed to shimmer; she had been breathing heavily, but now she had calmed down.

"It isn't about me, Publius. It never has been about me; it never will be." She drew near him, put her incorporeal hands on her shoulders, and touched them, but Publius could not feel anything; she was like a ghost or a phantasm, nothing more than an image in his mind.

Still, he stared into her eyes, and he knew she was staring back.

"You are near Paradise Gardens, Publius." Julia was smiling now, but it was a weary smile. She seemed beaten down, all her hopes and energy exhausted. She seemed almost defeated, but not quite. There was a kernel of strength still in her, a kernel of a life not yet over, a life that had to continue at least a little while longer. But Julia was strong; Publius knew her to be strong.

"Paradise Gardens," Publius repeated her words. "I have never been."

"Perhaps, nor should you," Julia said, "for it is a wealthy place, a place of opulence. But there is darkness there."

"There is darkness everywhere," Publius said.

"But there is darkness in some places more than others," Julia said.

Publius looked around; on these treeless hills, he could not make out a single soul. There was no gleam of banner or weapon, no trace of habitation. And so he found himself sitting down in the waning afternoon heat. He was exhausted.

Julia sat down next to him. Publius began to offer her his waterskin—women first—and then laughed, remembering she was nothing more than an apparition, an image only he could see. He slaked his thirst as best he could, emptying most of the remains. He prayed to the gods there would be some stream or pool, or some way to fill it, when he resumed his trek tomorrow.

He had about run out of food, but he helped himself to a bit of waybread.

Julia was looking at him, observing him, in a way he did not entirely like. Those eyes were full of wisdom, and they reflected a gentle soul, but they were examining, probing, weighing, judging.

"I'd offer you some food," Publius said, "but I don't think you'd eat it."

Julia smiled faintly. "Ah, Publius, it is good you are able to joke. I have been oppressed lately, so weighed down with what is coming on the world. I've had dizzy spells… I've felt faint. But you are my company… you are my comfort… when they—when them—"

Julia seemed to jerk back; she looked to her left.

She blinked from view, and Publius began to panic.

But she reappeared moments afterward. "Sorry," she said to him. "I thought they were coming."

In all this time, Julia had not mentioned a word about who her captors were, about who had plucked her from the Imperial Palace. Publius had asked before, but he had come to realize that she would never tell him, not as long as he lived.

"I am in danger," Julia said, "but I will be with you as long as I can. For as long as I am able."

She began to scan the hills. "Ah... this place... I do not recognize it. Are you sure you have been going due southwest?" she said.

"There are patrols everywhere," Publius said. "I've been trying to avoid them. I am in trouble with the military, you know."

"No," Julia said. "No. You will not be in trouble. For the Empire does not know of the Blighted Temple, or of the cult of the Blighted One.

"You are safe. The centurion was no centurion at all. He was a member of the cult and nothing more; he stole you from Blue Eagle Camp through deception. It was through false pretenses that he took the recruits out of the ranks."

Relief washed over him, but then he began to question her words. The centurion had been in full regalia. He had gone into the midst of the camp, promising to join up with the Second Anthanian Legion. And murder he had not committed, for he had killed in self-defense. But in the end he had committed a crime.

"Desertion," Publius said. "Punishable by death."

"No," Julia said, "not desertion; for I am sure, by now, the tribune of Blue Eagle Camp has learned the truth. You have committed no crime, Publius; you are innocent. I am a loyal servant of both the gods and the Empire. Would I tell you, as the emperor's daughter, to break the law?"

The relief returned, and something else filled his heart. As he peered into Julia's eyes, he wondered if he had it in him to disappoint her.

In the end he said the words. "Julia," Publius said, "I have grown to love you as a dear friend. But I am turning around. I am going back to Blue Eagle Camp. I have always wanted to join the legions, ever since I was a little boy."

It had not been his constant desire; it was a minor untruth. But he did want to join the legions now more than anything, and though he did love Julia, he had a life to live, and a country to serve.

"Well," Julia said, "I fear you will be disappointed in your choice. And I fear the world itself will suffer."

She blinked out of sight and Publius, again, was alone, suddenly filled with regret, suddenly filled with sadness.

Chapter Thirty-Three

Publius Allius Corvus

It was three days' walk, through many winding roads, before Publius reached Blue Eagle camp.

The recruits were there, stretching their legs before a drill, two-hundred in number, surrounded by tents.

Publius saw the tribune there, with a splendid iron helm on his head, and found himself begin to back away. He wondered of the truth of Julia's words, if she was right or wrong. What if she had just been some kind of ghost, some nefarious spirit leading him astray?

But he was a man; he had to conquer his fears.

He stepped forward, then proceeded at a walk.

The tribune shouted something and raised his hand. "Halt!" he said. His eyes met Publius' gaze. "Eh… go! Back to your quarters, everyone. I will see you in an hour."

The recruits did not disperse immediately. In confusion they hesitated, but the tribune waved his hand, and so they scurried this way and that, back to the tents that were their homes.

Publius took a few halting steps toward the tribune, and the tribune crossed the distance.

"Publius," he said. He was pallid and fat faced, with dark eyes to match his dark helmet. "You and the others… you were taken. But you came back. I will need you to return for questioning. We must understand what happened and why."

Chapter Thirty-Four

Agatho Lornodoris, Speaker of the Council

The Council had not met in several days.

The sun was shining in the heavens; the warmth was thick but not oppressive.

And Agatho had found himself in a place where he did not belonged, in the Imperial Palace whose power he had usurped.

The Council had passed a law, but the other side of government—where the powers of military command, foreign affairs and the settling of disputes traditionally resided—still had a say. The Imperial Council, having claimed those powers until a candidate for the White Throne was identified, still had to meet with the various officials and ministers.

And so it was Agatho wandering through those halls, yes, Agatho, through the nest of vipers called the Imperial Palace. He was a hated man there, now, but even he knew that this was temporary, that the Council could not command the Empire forever.

The narrow corridors and dim lit hallways took him at last to the Vespers Wing where—behind an open door, as expected— the Magister of War was sitting.

Behind his desk a red gold Imperial flag was displayed, and light was filtering in through the windows above it. Throughout the room, which was faced with white marble, various emblems of the military were displayed: medals of fallen soldiers, a bust of Anthans with a laurel wreath upon his head, and even a gold eagle standard fitted to a flag.

"Lornodoris," the Magister said, "welcome to the palace."

His resentment bubbled over, oozing from each word, from each syllable. Contempt for the Council had grown as the powers of the Imperial Palace waned. In the early days of the Empire, most power resided in the arms of the Council, but with each passing generation that was less and less true. The emperor was beginning to resemble a king in his own right, though his powers—according to law—arose from the Councilors. Much had been lost over these years, much power and much wisdom, but Lornodoris never let a crisis go to waste. As the Empire showed cracks, he would reinvigorate the people's assembly. He would reinvigorate the Council.

"Greetings, Magister," Agatho said.

As the Speaker of the Council he would not deign to sit. But the Magister of War, by name Lucius Alcibiades, had called him in and he would respond to the inquiries of his subordinates.

"I have called you here to speak of the Ugar Coast," the Magister said.

The First Ugar War had taken place twenty years prior. The cities of the northwestern coastlands, founded on rich soil, had been eyed for millennia. They were a foreign culture to the peninsula, contrasting strongly with the the native Geats of the east and the Eloesian city-states of the southwest.

The war, begun after the city of Tikal called for aid, had ended in an uneasy peace. The cities of the coast had largely become Friends of the Empire—a term of legal weight, ensuring Imperial protection—all except Eioli, who refused.

"The war has not gone as expected," Lornodoris said.

"No," the Magister said, "it has not. And as the Speaker of the Council, you now bear the Imperium of the White Throne. It is your task to lead the people's armies in war."

Lornodoris felt a smile coming upon him, one he had not expected.

In his youth in Paradise Gardens, he had resisted the call of Grand Legate and Master of the Horse. He had feared war, and now in his old age it was a point of mockery at dinner parties.

Finally, he could put them in their place, and at a distance.

"I will go to Eioli," Lornodoris said. "I will lead the people's armies, as is my duty."

What resistance could a band of primitives put up? Armed with crude spears, they would break upon the might of the Imperial Legions.

And the Council, in the process, would regain its glory.

The Empire had strayed since the Unification. But Lornodoris would bring it back to its ideals.

"To Eioli I go," Lornodoris said. "Send the word. Prepare a war chariot."

Chapter Thirty-Five

Publius Allius Corvus

The days had not been easy since returning to Blue Eagle Camp.

The drills had begun again, and Publius had rejoined them, but old problems resurfaced, old hurts and old resentments. Other recruits were advancing faster; other recruits showed more skill with the sword, and when Publius strayed in his formation the tribune was quick to belittle him.

And as for what happened in the mountains, it was as if the tribune had forgotten; but Publius knew he had not forgotten. The tribune said nothing about the incident, about the "centurion" who had shown his face, but Publius had told him everything he knew, about the mountain road, about the arduous trek, about the black stone temple nestled in a high valley. When he told the tribune he had received a blank stare, a confused look, and little more.

The old resentments returned, and Julia was gone.

As Publius followed his fellow recruits' lead up and down hills and through obstacles, he wondered if he had made a mistake. The soldier's life was not easy; it was not meant to be easy. Julia had promised him something more, a different purpose, a different goal; but now she no longer appeared to him. She had rejected him, and he her. He wondered if he would ever see her again.

But whether he would or wouldn't no longer mattered. From dawn to dusk he trained, with sword, with shield, running, driving himself to exhaustion, wondering at the end of each day whether it was all worth it, whether even the Empire was worth fighting for.

And at night he would dream terrible dreams about the black temple and the dark-robed cultists within. He did not understand and he did not want to understand. He did not want to think about it, yet whenever he fell asleep the visions would come, the visions formed from frightful memories. He would look at his right hand and think of the knife he once held, the knife which he had plunged into the "centurion's" heart.

There was word of trouble on the Ugar Coast, though the tribune told the recruits very little. Publius knew there was an operation underway there.

Yes, he had heard the politicians' justifications. When he first signed up for the army, he had overheard a speech from his councilor, Sixtus Valerius, that the war against Eioli was a justified one. But he had begun to doubt the longer the war went on. Should the Empire force a city into its fold? What if the city resisted, if its citizens did not want it? What, then? Was the war justified?

Up the hill he sprinted. The group leader shouted "Stop!" and in the next moment raised his hand, a signal to shift into formation.

The strongest recruits hurried to the front of the group and knelt downward, raising their arms as if they bore shields. Publius was in the second line of the shield formation, behind his partner Tychus. He raised his hand as if his shield were above him.

Within the span of moments, the tortoise formation had formed, and the group leader shouted something else. Soon they were marching forth at a slow pace, imagining Ugars or northern barbarians in front of them. The march of the legions was slow, but it was overpowering, and few could overcome it. A century of men, with locked shields, was virtually impossible to stop, lurching forward like a juggernaut, pressing ahead like an unstoppable titan. It was the Empire's method of war that many tried to copy but none succeeded at.

The barbarians of the north were individualistic in their combat, flinging themselves into battle without strategy or forethought. The Ugars of the coast were cowards by nature, hiring mercenaries and avoiding battle but fighting like cornered rats when there was no other choice. Neither could stand against the legion, shields locked together, shields ahead and shields above, marching forth, trampling ahead, crushing all before it.

The group leader stood up. The recruits relaxed.

The sun was beating down on the barren hills, and the air was wavering in the heat. Publius again thought of Julia, as was his wont. He missed her so.

~

The sun was setting. The heat had begun to sink into Publius, radiating through every sinew, every inch of his body, and though the night was coming he knew he would never shake it. He wanted winter to come, yes, winter, the cold, the darkness, the rain.

They had regrouped at Blue Eagle Camp and the tribune was there. He was waiting for them, and the hundreds of other recruits had surrounded him.

"Men of Blue Eagle camp," the commandant said. "Many of you have shown promise in these summer months. I have no doubt some of you will become full legionaries. You have a fortnight of rest, under supervision, in the town of Tres Taberna. You will return to Blue Eagle camp to continue your training on the first of Sextil."

Sextil, the month that was synonymous with heat in Imperial City, was a time that common citizens dreamed of getting away. Publius was in the cool of the foothills, where a gentle wind blew and banished the worst of the warmth. But what wouldn't he give to be back in his old haunt, yes, even in Mud Bottom, one of Imperial City's most impoverished wards. The heat would be agonizing, and even the dogs would lie there panting, but Publius wanted to be there, away from Blue Eagle Camp, away from the trouble, away—especially—from the Blighted Temple and its dark memories.

He had forgotten about the coming summer break, a two week respite for recruits to regain their strength. It had been a taxing few months, for Publius more than anyone else.

He still did not understand what happened to him. Perhaps he never would.

But for now, the town of Tres Taberna called.

Chapter Thirty-Six

Publius Allius Corvus

The town of Tres Taberna faced the sea. A gentle breeze was blowing when Publius ended his journey. The air smelled of salt and a fog was rolling in from the sea in a vapor.

It was a large town, large enough and more to handle the arrival of the Blue Eagle Camp, but Publius did not know if it was well provisioned enough to suit their drinking.

Publius had never been much fond of drink, but in the weeks he'd been at Blue Eagle he had heard little talk of anything but wine and women.

These two weeks were good for the bones, but Publius worried they'd be bad for the mind, for all he could think about, waking or sleeping, was Julia and her task, and the memory of what had happened to him.

~

The homes and shops of Tres Taberna were shingled with red tile, and the outer walls were layered with bright white plaster. It seemed there was a garden in every home, and among its winding streets there appeared to be few people. Publius found himself walking alone, away from the recruits he hardly knew. He had spent so much time with them, but he felt he did not truly know them; he felt he did not truly connect. And so here he was, walking the quaint streets of Tres Taberna, not knowing what to do, not knowing how to spend his hours.

Eventually, his walk took him to the edge of the town, to a small harbor where fisher's boats bobbed up and down. There was a stone square surrounded by ivy-covered buildings, and the remains of fish stands and vendors were there, long after the sellers went home.

The sun was setting in the west, and behind him the sky was aflame with red and gold colors. He thought of Julia. He looked to the sea and saw its waves. He said aloud, "Julia, Julia… hear me…"

But there was no sign of her, no propitious wind, no shaft of light, no miraculous appearance. Julia was nowhere to be found. But in his heart, Publius felt he would see her soon, that she would not abandon him.

He had resisted her once; could he, now, again?

He had two weeks, an extended break from his training, a break that—for most—was necessary, with torn ligaments, aching muscles, and above all a worn down spirit. But for him, he felt this period would not be a break of any kind, but in fact a source of stress.

For something had happened to him, something he could not explain. Julia, the emperor's daughter, had been appearing to him in a ghostlike state, in a state that only he could see.

He had rejected her request, and that rejection would weigh heavy on him.

Why did she want him to go to Saturnus Rock and say "The Red Lord cometh?" What could it mean? What did she know?

Chapter Thirty-Seven

Publius Allius Corvus

Night had set, and the winds were churning the sea. The moon was out, but clouds were moving swiftly, veiling it and unveiling it in rapid succession. Publius had a feeling it would be one of those rare summer storms.

The recruits of Blue Eagle camp, or more specifically the recruits of the Black Century, had set up a party spot of sorts on the harbor. Barrels of wine had been ferried out, and on the stone a fire had been made, where shanks of lamb and cuts of beef were sizzling.

Lucius was there, the person Publius had grown closest to. He was from Imperial City like Publius; unlike Publius he was a man of esteem, hailing from Canal District, from a merchant family of the Knightly class. The soldier's life had not been necessary for him; it had been a choice.

They had been the closest of friends after Publius first began his training, but now, in the wake of all that had gone on, there had been a distance opening up between them. For Publius, there had been a distance with everyone since he had met Julia, a distance he could not bridge, a distance he felt deep inside his heart, almost an emptiness.

Lucius was pouring himself a cup of wine. Like the other recruits, his hair was closely cropped. Publius' was too, though he had allowed his to grow a little overlong, and traces of a beard were starting to emerge on his chin. By custom, legionaries were clean shaven, with hair cut short.

"Why aren't you drinking?" Lucius said.

Publius didn't know what to tell him. Could he tell him that he missed someone dear to him, someone he almost thought he loved? Would Lucius believe him if he said the emperor's daughter had appeared to him in a dream, from a great distance and only he could see him?

In the end, Publius' answer was to go to the barrel, empty cup in hand, and fill it with the bubbling red liquid. He tasted it, though he hadn't wanted to drink anything, and found it was as he expected, a watered down and poor quality wine that only grunts could endure. But such wine, in large quantities, could make you drunk, and that, he supposed, was the goal of his fellow recruits, even if it wasn't his.

"Why am I not drinking?" Publius said, cup in hand, and took a light sip. "What do you have to say for yourself now?"

Lucius had begun to smile. In Imperial City, a poor young man like Publius might be looked down upon, but in the ranks of the legion there was no poor or rich, no Knight or common. In such a setting, Publius was Lucius' peer.

Lucius was walking away, and Publius began to follow him.

He followed him around the edge of the harbor, beside the waters twinkling with moonlight. The oppressive heat of the day had all but evaporated, and the gentle wind was cold, as exhilarating as it was refreshing. Publius had not been relieved to depart Blue Eagle Camp, but now he was, at least in some ways.

"You've changed," Lucius said.

It was a pointed thing to say, verging on rudeness, but it was a sign that Lucius considered him a close friend.

"…ever since…"

"I left?" Publius said, finishing the thought for him. "Well, Lucius, if I told you what I'd seen… if I told you what had happened, I don't think you'd believe me."

"Try me," Lucius said.

There were some things you shouldn't say, some dark

places you shouldn't go. And what Publius had seen he still did not understand, he still could not comprehend. Julia and her request, the temple in the mountains, the false centurion… it still made little sense. They were like little pieces of a puzzle Publius couldn't quite put together, and the more he mashed them around, the more he tried to connect the hard edges, the less clear the puzzle's image was.

"I was led," Publius said, "into the mountains. We traveled for weeks."

"The Goldenhorns?" Lucius said.

"Yes," Publius replied.

The Goldenhorns marked the eastern edges of the peninsula; they stretched into the wild lands of the barbarian north.

"And it was hard going," Publius said.

"I would imagine," Lucius answered.

Publius did not want to tell him everything; in truth, he didn't want to tell him anything. But he had to tell him something, a faint morsel of it, a small part of it that wasn't deception. "And," Publius said, "I was lied to. The 'centurion' wasn't a centurion at all. I escaped one night… I don't know what happened to the others."

"And how did you find out it was a lie?" Lucius said.

Publius almost said "Julia," but stopped himself. It was she who had told him; it was she whom he owed his life to. And now she was nowhere to be found. But she would come back soon—that was what Publius told himself.

Julia, Julia… he thought of her when the breeze buffeted him from the sea, he thought of her, of her blue eyes and her golden hair, when he woke up in the morning and when he went to bed at night. He wondered if refusing her request had been a mistake; he wondered if he should have indeed gone to Saturnus Rock, if he should have risked everything and uttered those inexplicable words, "The Red Lord Cometh."

"How did I find out the centurion lied?" Publius said. "I... I... I don't know."

Lucius was a friend, but he was not that close of a friend. Publius knew the recruits of the Black Century; he knew they would mock him ceaselessly, like they had mocked others.

"I guess," Publius said, "I was led to believe it somehow. I was led to doubt..."

If he had gone through with Julia's request, he could have seen her in the mornings and in the evenings. But the legion offered pay, and free food. It offered some semblance of a future, though one that was fraught with risks and uncertainty.

"Well, you haven't seemed the same," Lucius said. "I hope you get back to your old self."

Lucius wandered away, and this time Publius did not follow. The waves were crashing in on the rocks, and the moonlight shimmered upon them. The air smelled of salt and fish and detritus. The shores on the eastern edge of the peninsula were surprisingly deep, and the natives—in the time before the Imperials arrived—worshiped a god called Orkus, the lord of sharks and sea jellies. It was said they would take sacrificial victims—yes, sacrificial victims—and tie an anchor around their leg, and drop them into the depths. He wondered how many souls had perished that way, according to that barbaric custom.

"Julia," he whispered to the crashing seas. "Julia... come back to me..."

The winds seemed to pick up, and the waves began to wax in size. Soon they were crashing heavily over the rocks, spraying even Publius—high above—with foam. He saw Julia in the foam, in the wan moonlight. He saw her in the stars, those brilliant beacons that guided sailors far out to sea. He saw her everywhere, and in his mind she was dancing and laughing, beckoning him to come close.

Julia, the emperor's daughter, had once appeared to him...

but where was she now?

Chapter Thirty-Eight

Tidus Sulpicius Varro, Marshal of the Guard

The Speaker of the Council, Agatho Lornodoris, had dismissed Varro; he had sent him away. And so it was the palace and not a person that Varro guarded.

He was walking through the hallways when he remembered the emissary from afar, telling him to find the "Star of Seladora."

Magisters and palace slaves were scurrying to and fro, but Varro had halted his walk. He had paused, remembering the so-called "Star of Seladora"—a family heirloom of the Seánus family. It was a gem that seemed to sparkle in the sunlight, so much that it was called a star.

In the days since Lornodoris rejected him, Varro had spent his time—whenever he could, at the best possible moments—searching for the star. He told no one about this quest, for he hadn't approached it with seriousness. But now, watching magisters run about, those who were entrusted with matters of war or commerce or even silly positions such as the Guardian of the Wine Cabinet, he realized it was no worse a use of his time.

The Imperial Palace was a place of busybodies, and many magisters on the public payroll did very little work at all, spending their time at parties and enjoying the perks of their positions. Why shouldn't Varro chase this elusive rabbit, this Star of Seladora, which an emissary had told him about?

It had been in his hands once, that talisman that he now sought. It was that talisman, crushed and trodden underfoot, that had proven Julia's kidnapping. It was that talisman that had proven, once and for all, as clear as daylight, that something terrible had befallen the Imperial family.

And then, in a matter of weeks, worse had happened... the

emperor himself had been killed, murdered by assassins at an opportune moment.

Varro bore a small bit of responsibility, but his absence had been at the emperor's command; the emperor had demanded he uncover the cult of the Red Hand. Now, the assassins who had killed the emperor were finally talking; transported to the shores of an allied city where Imperial law did not apply, those assassins—Imperial citizens both—were being tortured at the behest of the King of Kheroe. They would unveil the truth about the Red Hand, and name its members. In foreign lands, Imperial laws were not relevant. That was what the Empire had allies for.

The hallway was grand, and the Imperial palace itself was like a beehive, with rooms and corridors stretching every which way. Varro recalled showing the emperor the Star of Seladora in his bedchamber. That bedchamber was now empty; and even if Speaker Lornodoris was present, he still—by law—was not allowed to use it. The Council had usurped much of the palace's power, but certain customs were to be observed, and certain laws were sacrosanct. The bedchamber would be empty, and Varro—by right of his position—was allowed to enter. If he could not find the Star of Seladora there, perhaps he'd find something that would lead to it.

~

The bedchamber was locked but Varro had the keys. When he opened it, there was a musty smell.

Haunting, it was, a place of such regal splendor that was now abandoned. It was like the emperor had departed and a ghost had arrived in his place. The windows, of gold-colored silk, were flapping in the breeze; the main hall, lined with fine Fharese carpets, was empty. On a table of teak, there was an empty wine glass.

Emperor Seánus had been a good leader, the finest of his

kind. The troops had adored him, and he had worked his way up through the ranks of the military. When he sent the Imperial forces to war, they would do so gladly, because Seánus had been on the front lines himself. It was a rarity for a nobleman; and now the cowardly, servile creatures of the Imperial Council, where every matter was debated ad nauseum to no end, had seized the levers of power. The Imperial Council could not be trusted with finances or passing good laws; yet they were so full of themselves, seeing no one worthy to appoint as emperor, but so arrogant as to think they could rule in his place.

"Marcus Seánus," Varro said to the empty room, "your people miss you. And so do I."

Augusts, Knights, common, it did not matter. Marcus was a rarity; a true nobleman among those who did not deserve the term. His daughter had been the most pious woman Varro ever met, a young woman of infinite moral character. And now they had been taken from their nation, replaced by a council of thirty conniving serpents. All authority, in theory, came from the Imperial Council, from the representatives of the free men of the city. But there were customs and laws and regulations; there were precedents, and though it was legal, perhaps, in theory, for the Council to seize power in cases of emergencies, it troubled Varro; it troubled everyone.

"Star of Seladora," Varro said, as if it were sentient, as if it could call out and tell him where it was.

"Star of Seladora!" Varro said, a little louder, though he knew it was mad. He walked into the bedroom, where fine silken sheets lay over golden pillows. Outside the bedroom, a window looked down many fathoms below to the red roofs and twisted streets of the city.

Varro searched the desk, finding only odd trinkets and a smattering of coins. Hanging near the door was the Seánus family sword, which Marcus had carried in battle.

There were portraits of his father, an old miser, with a younger Marcus—dressed in child-sized armor—kneeling ahead of him.

Seánus, Lornodoris, Kerius: family names that held such high esteem. But Varro—though he was not noble—had seen them in person, closer than the common ever would. He saw that they were people and people only, and in any family there are bad apples, twisted branches off the family tree. Marcus had been the greatest of the nobles in Varro's estimation, a man whose legacy would live on long after his death. Varro would cherish his memory; if and when he found the Star of Seladora, he would return it to Marcus' closest remaining relative.

Only a woman's word of sooth was the cause, but he endeavored to find it, if he could at all.

He searched the bedroom, looking even under the rug, and then in the great wardrobe which was a separate room in and of itself. Now, the racks of clothing were empty, and it was more spacious than Varro had ever seen it. The whole room was haunting, for usually, before an emperor died, there was a designated successor, and as soon as he gave up the ghost the Imperial Council would vote him in.

Now, as with the Empire itself, the bedroom was missing its emperor, the ruler who had been given power since the beginning, since the time of the Unification. Unworthy men had succeeded him, thirty doddering, senile fools who only knew how to argue and to disagree. The Empire was in peril; and though the Red Hand assassins had been caught, other threats had arisen—a failed siege in Eioli, unrest in the city streets, and far beyond, in the barbarian north, a rumor of war. Many remembered the day when the sky had turned red; and everywhere there was a note of dolour and omen. Would the end come? Many had expected it before, and yet the world endured.

The wardrobe was empty; cobwebs were in the corners.

He remembered presenting the Star of Seladora, which had been broken and trodden underfoot, to the Imperial Council. Would that house of fools have laid their hands on it? They were known to seize property from citizens at random; could they also have seized the Seánus family star?

~

But he searched the Imperial Council House – or at least, what rooms he was allowed to access in that maze of hidden chambers and secret doors – and there was nothing there. Only marble floors and whitewashed walls, bronze statues and stone busts greeted him.

Varro fell to sleep that night in his private chambers, and he dreamed, yes, he dreamed, of the goddess Seladora. Around her neck a necklace had been laid, and in that center of the necklace was a star pulsing with light. Then he looked up at the goddess's face but saw it was not the goddess at all, but it was a woman wearing the star, a woman with blonde hair and blue eyes, with luscious red lips… the emperor's daughter, Julia.

"Where is it?" she said. "Where is my star?"

Chapter Thirty-Nine

Publius Allius Corvus

The days had passed slowly, and the nights had been difficult.

In the town of Tres Taberna, where he was supposedly in the midst of two weeks of rest, he had been offered better lodgings than ever. He was staying at a fine inn; he was sharing a room with his friend Lucius. But in the mornings he would find himself wandering off, isolating himself from his fellow recruits, thinking not of the training ahead of him or the hopes of a lucrative legionary's career, but of what he had seen, what he had witnessed.

What indeed was the black temple? What indeed was that dark mountain road? And how had Julia found him? She claimed she could project herself onto others, appear before them as if she were a ghost or a wraith… but how had she found Publius? How did she know where he was walking? If she could visit the spirit world, then why did she choose Publius? Why, of all people, did she project herself onto him?

In the harbor, the winds were tossing up the gray waves, which were crashing onto rocks. There was a chill wind blowing. In the distance, he could hear the laughter of his fellow recruits, rising above the din of the fishmongers who were just now starting to sell the catch of the day.

He scanned the gray clouds; he breathed in the salt air of the coast. There was only a little while left, and then he would return to his training.

The legionary's salary would perhaps make him forget all this. When he was posted in some foreign country, or tasked with guarding the border, when he had a wife and three children depending on him in Imperial City, perhaps he would forget all this.

Perhaps it would all be behind him.

Perhaps it would all be behind him.

Chapter Forty

Varro, Marshal of the Guard

The Council was approaching the end of its self-appointed term at the White Throne.

In absentia of an emperor, they could rule indefinitely; but Varro doubted they would break tradition with such violence. In the past, such terms of Council rule had gone on as long as six months, but no longer. And Varro would guard whoever they appointed; it was his duty for life.

The halls of the Imperial Palace had grown quieter now; there was less life and busyness. In the Anthans Corridor where he was walking, marble statues were the only faces that greeted him, white likenesses of early Imperial statesmen and Eastern philosophers. The tile was a chipped beige, the ceilings and walls a crimson edged with gold. It was a spacious hallway, a place of reflection on history's great men, a place where the former emperor Marcus—the only one truly worthy of the White Throne—liked to walk, and think, and strategize. Varro knew; he had walked with Marcus in this place before.

But it was different now; Varro was alone, and the Imperial Palace was alone, without a guiding head. In the place of one strong leader thirty bickering cowards had assumed control.

A shadow appeared in the distance, on the far side of the hall, between the statues of Hordo and Ansolon. It was a lithe figure, tall yet slight, a woman. And in the flickering lights of lamps he could make out a fur coat, a trace of blonde hair.

Varro by now had frozen, whether in fear or something else he did not know. He was waiting there, not knowing what to say or do, not knowing how to respond. The Imperial Palace was not open to visitors, and it was his task to arrest and carry away interlopers.

And yet… who was that standing there? There was no trace of anxiety in her, no worry about being caught. And yet, though she was familiar, she seemed out of place to Varro, and utterly so.

Varro was a simple man; he did not cause trouble unless it was asked for. He would not allow this in any other circumstance; and yet he remained there standing.

"Who goes there?" he finally worked up the gumption to say.

"Is an official member of the palace not allowed to walk the Anthans corridor?" she said. "Have things changed since I was here last?"

The voice was familiar, but foreign. Where had he heard it before?

Goose bumps had formed over Varro's chest, and if it weren't for his military training, he'd be the one backing off, stepping away, giving ground to this bold intruder. He had a sword… oh, why was he thinking of using a sword? He was afraid now, and true; and yet he managed to stay put, to put on a brave face, to give no hint of the anxiety that was building within him.

Then it dawned on him, the fur, the coat, the blonde hair, the blue eyes and the dark outline of lips.

"Julia!" Varro shouted and as he ran to her the anxieties, worries and fears melted away into nothing.

He had found her, but not by his own hand. He had answered the riddle, but not by his own efforts.

As he ran the whole of the corridor, her image became clear, and her blue eyes were twinkling, and she was smiling. He rushed up to her, put a hand on her cloak… and watched as it passed straight through the fur, as if she were a ghost or a spirit and nothing more, a picture made from vapor.

The fear returned a hundredfold; his heart was racing.

"What is this?" Varro said. "what devilry is this?

"Have you died and returned to life, Julia? Are you a

revenant? Who killed you? Tell me, so I can put a sword through their throat."

But Julia's blue eyes twinkled all the more, and her lips curled into a smile brighter than before. "I am not dead, Varro. I am alive, in fact, more alive than I have ever been."

He remembered the words of Marcus at that moment, the words of the emperor that—at the time—had seemed liked delusion, like madness. He had claimed his daughter had supernatural powers, that she could appear to him at will, from great distances. What had Marcus called it? He had called it "projection."

"Julia," Varro found himself saying. It seemed it was all he could say. "Julia… Julia…"

And though she was insubstantial, just an image or a vapor, Varro continued to try to brush her, to continue to try to touch her.

"Julia… you must tell me where you are," Varro said.

He had not believed Marcus at first; the talk of "projection" and celestial bodies had seemed like something a madman would say, something you'd hear from a foaming-at-the-mouth beggar on an Imperial City street. Now… well, now, he saw it for himself, and if there was madness involved he was seeing it too.

"Where I am, you can't go," Julia said, "because they would find you. They would hear you coming… then they would kill us both."

"But you can tell me who took you," Varro said. "I was supposed to protect you. I am Tidus Sulpicius Varro, Marshal of the Guard. You were my charge. And so was your father… ah, my dear, have you not heard? News does not travel easily to captives. Your father… your father… he has passed on."

Julia's eyes began to water; her smile vanished and her mouth fell agape. "Surely not, Varro. You must be kidding. My father! My father? When you are a little girl, you think your parents will never die but… but…"

"You must tell me who took you!" Varro said. "I will be careful not to alert them. But you must tell me, Julia. Were they barbarians? Smugglers? Pirates from the Gold Coast?"

"Varro," Julia said. She had wiped her eyes, and her voice no longer trembled. "I cannot tell you what you want to hear. I wish I could, but I cannot.

"Instead a task I ask of you," Julia said. "A task that is simple, but one that will lead to my rescue. I cannot explain it.

"Varro, take my star. It is in a shelf in the Council House, in the Speaker's chambers, with a lock that does not work."

How did she know this? Varro supposed, in her ethereal state, she knew much; that she could walk the halls of the palace and the Council House undetected, even from far away.

"Take my star, Varro," Julia said. "Take it… Then, go to Saturnus Rock. Declare in your loudest voice 'The Red Lord cometh!' And then your task will be done."

Chapter Forty-One

Publius Allius Corvus

It was late summer, and in the dense heat the air wavered.

Blue Eagle camp was in sight, but it had changed. The tents had been all torn down, and on metal prongs many suits of armor gleamed in the sun, helmets polished like mirrors with great red horsehair crests. They were the armor of full legionaries, men who had passed their training and then gone on to receive their reward, their payment, their salary, their career.

The tribune was there and so were several others. They were in full regalia, and as leaders of the legion the horsehair crests of their helms were sideways.

Publius couldn't believe his eyes. Those were fine suits of armor, made of gleaming metal.

Before, the false centurion had lied to him, but now he saw real, true armor, and beside them were swords.

He had only been training for six months. In the best of circumstances, taking up the arms of the legion took nine.

"Greetings, green recruits of Blue Eagle Camp," the tribune said. "You were due to achieve full status in a matter of a year, but your country needs you. In the west of this peninsula, I am sure you have heard… the Ugar city of Eioli has defied our emissaries. And it is your task to bring the Empire's peace to the peninsula, to ensure our children have a future.

"Each one of you has been granted the rank of legionary. Into the legions you will go, starting in the morning. Your assignments will be given you at dawn.

"Go, recruits of Blue Eagle Camp. Don your armor. Eioli waits."

Chapter Forty-Two

Agatho Lornodoris, Speaker of the Council, Commander-in-Chief

It was late summer and the cicadas were chirping.

Agatho's carriage came to a sudden halt; the jarring, bumpy ride had ended abruptly.

"Signor Lornodoris!" he heard his guard proclaim. "We are here, at Forward Camp."

Agatho was no man of military rank; he had no experience with the sword or horse. But he was a politician. He knew how to put on a good show.

He got up, brushed his tunic, adjusted his purple sash, and opened the door.

He stepped out into the blazing heat to find a sprawling collection of tents.

For a military camp, the staging ground of the Ugar campaign, he could not help but note the lack of people.

And by some of the tents were men, perhaps legionaries, sitting on the ground, quaking and chattering.

"Forward Camp," he said. "I have never felt so at home."

Interlude II

"The Ugars are coming!" some in Imperial City said. "They will kill us all!"

And indeed, the rumors had frightened those in the streets, for the city entirely lacked walls. There were reports of a great army of mercenaries, of wild beasts and elephants and monstrous men, that had broken the legions and was stampeding southwards.

But worse was going on, and overall the talk was not largely of this difficult-to-believe and probably false rumor.

For the children of Imperial City were dreaming dark dreams, and some were plunging themselves into fires. There were reports of shaking and babbling—the divine disease—and of men growing horns on their heads.

"It is the end of the world," some said, but others said they'd thought that before.

Remember, said they, the evening when the skies turned blood red, and the next day the waters were still and blue?

Chapter Forty-Three

Tidus Sulpicius Varro, Marshal of the Guard

Varro was a man of logic and reason. But he would also do anything for Julia.

He was riding alone on his horse when Saturnus Rock came into view.

It was shaped like an anvil, black, basalt, an immense monolith that overlooked the coast.

And Varro saw that he was not alone.

He clutched the trampled Star of Seladora to his chest and brought his horse to a halt.

What was happening?

Hundreds were gathered here, here on the coast battered by waves. The fog obscured them but their clothing was crimson, and out of the maritime vapors Varro made out faces... one the woman from before, the emissary from "Pelagios," Isadora. She was no Easterner, but a fraud.

"What is this?" Varro cried.

His horse reared up onto her hind legs and whinnied. But for all the beast bothering him, he was afraid too, a worry growing in the pit of his stomach, a distinct sense of unease.

And then he heard her voice.

Julia was walking out from among the crowds. She too was garbed in red. Her blue eyes were radiant as ever. She was here in the body, here, among these Red Hand cultists. She had not been captive; she had lied to Varro and to her father. It was she who dropped her star, she who trampled it underfoot to make things seem amiss.

"Julia!" Varro said. "Your father would be disappointed in you."

"My father is gone," Julia said. "Dismount, Varro! Meet me!"

Varro found himself doing just that. For all her deceptions, he could not help but guard Julia; he could not help but protect her.

He walked over to her, touched her arm. Sure enough she was here in the flesh; she was no ghostly apparition but a real person.

"Lay my star around my neck," Julia said.

She was the emperor's daughter, or at least she had been. He laid the gold cord around her neck, and even in the fog the star seemed to fluoresce.

"Say the words," Julia said. "Say the words you told me you would say."

But this time Varro resisted, for his loyalty was not infinite, his love for her was not undying.

"Say them!" Julia said again, and this time, spurred by urgency, Varro blurted them out.

"The Red Lord cometh!" Varro shouted.

Trumpets pealed, dozens of trumpets in unison.

Out of the fog Maria Domina came marching, bearing a cloak and something else—a wreath.

She laid the red cloak over his shoulders and buttoned it below the neck. On his head she laid a wreath of red ivy and pine cones.

"The Red Lord has appeared," Maria Domina said. "And when he appears, the earth shall quake!"

There were cheers and there was dancing as Varro's horror grew. But then he peered into Julia's happy eyes. He would do anything for Julia Seánus... anything.

Part Three

Chapter Forty-Four

Constantius Pello, Speaker in Absentia

The morning sun was shining down from the Council House's oculus.

The thirty, now twenty-nine councilors were meeting for the first time in days.

"Men of the Council," Constantius said, and walked to the center of the room. *"Numera!"*

Constantius was not a rigid lover of tradition, but as Lornodoris's replacement, he thought he ought to give the rules and traditions of the Imperial Council the same weight.

From the shadows between the seats the Legis emerged, garbed in finery.

"One," he counted. "Two…"

He ended in the twenties and the Council was legally convened.

Into the center of the room beneath the oculus, Constantius strode, and he felt the sunlight touch upon his hair. "Tidings I bring to you," Constantius said.

They would not like the news.

"The cities of Avrit, Tikal and Hoda have revoked their status as Friends of the Empire," Constantius said. "I believe they are emboldened by Eioli's success, success we must quickly squash. But such an action has never been done before. It is without precedent. The city of Lornatium is a Friend of the Empire. What if, tomorrow, at high noon, the archon of Lornatium revokes his city's status? What if he too is emboldened by the rebellion? What then shall we tell him? There is no law, and now we are faced with the unthinkable. Friends revoking their Friendship. I yield the floor."

Constantius withdrew to the edge of the room; as the Speaker in Absentia, he had no assigned seat, and when other councilors would speak he would merely get out of their way. It was the way the Council operated; it was how the Council had conducted its business in the beginning, in the time before the Unification, when two tribes fought each other on a forgotten isle.

Out of the seats a figure emerged, the oldest of the Council, a senior member of the body named Lychicus who represented the city's western bounds. "I move to speak," Lychicus said, and Constantius was quick to answer.

"Your request is granted," Constantius said.

With a cane, Lychicus navigated the steps, grumbling inscrutable curses as he made his way to the center of the room. The light from the oculus shone upon his wrinkles and upon his bad left eye which was a shade of white. He was ancient, and if he claimed he had been in the Council since its founding it would not be hard to believe.

"Friends," Lychicus said, "Imperials. Augusts all.

"The Ugars are savages. Savages, they are! They must be taught a lesson, and so too must all who take advantage of our protection and our friendship. Our Friendship is not without a price. A price must be paid, and when services are given they must receive reward. When we crush the Ugars, and crush them we will, we must make an example of them.

"The Ugars are obstinate. And I move, friends, Imperials, Augusts, that we not allow our Friendship to lapse without payment. I call to bring them back into our fold, willingly or unwillingly. I move, that on the cities of the Ugar Coast, Eioli, Avrit, Tikal, Hoda, that we carry Imperial justice to them. I move that we declare war."

"Objection," said Saius, councilor from East Fork. He spoke with calmness, quietness, near silence. Lychicus was respected by all. As the oldest in the councilor, he was revered, and to treat him harshly was anathema.

The Legis walked forth. "Granted."

Mumbling curses, Lychicus turned around and hobbled up the steps. But in addition to being a harsh man, he was a respecter of tradition, of rules and precedent.

Saius took Lychicus' place in the center of the Council House, beneath the oculus. He was blond haired and wore his hair too long; some called it the mark of a barbarian. But he was confident, the councilor from East Fork; yes, he was.

"I move, friends, countrymen, Imperials, Augusts all, that we do not even dignify the revocation of status," Saius said. "I move that they have not left, because they cannot leave the fold. I move that they never revoked their status, because a Friend of the Empire must remain so until the Empire falls, or the world itself ends."

"And what, then, shall we do? Shall we pretend that all is well?" hissed Council Valerius of Mud Bottom.

"Order," Constantius said. He had learned the job of speaker was little more than referee. "Let the councilor from East Fork speak."

Saius smiled, stiffened his body. The oculus shone on his blond hair. He looked as one that was favored by the gods.

"No," Saius said. "We will not pretend that all is well. We will not pretend that our enemies do not resist us. We will enforce this body's decree, this body's ruling, that Friendship with the Empire may never be revoked. We will declare war, not just on Eioli, but on Eioli, Avrit, Tikal, and Hoda. I move, countrymen, Imperials, Augusts all, that we declare war on all the cities of the coast."

"Seconded!" Lychicus shouted.

"Thirded!" shouted another councilor.

Saius turned and walked back up toward the seat.

The Legis returned to the center of the room. In the corner, a clerk was furiously recording the morning's deliberations.

"Let the Speaker call the vote," the Legis said, "to declare war on the cities of the Ugar Coast, and that Friendship with the Empire—once agreed to—may never be revoked."

Constantius strode forward. "The speaker votes aye."

~

In the end, the vote was twenty-nine to none. The Council had finally agreed on something unanimously.

And war was coming, whether the people of the Empire wanted it or not.

Chapter Forty-Five

Agatho Lornodoris, Speaker of the Council, Grand Legate

Four legions had been placed under Lornodoris' command.

The weight of it hung heavy over him as he wandered amongst the tents of Forward Camp.

He was no soldier, and of strategy he had only a passing grasp of things. But when they finally brought Eioli into submission, he'd be called a hero, and perhaps a triumphal procession was in order, a parade of soldiers marching down the way, with Lornodoris at its head.

Lornodoris passed slowly through the camp.

He did not want his nerves to get the best of him.

When the Magister of War had explained the situation, he had thought it a golden opportunity.

But now, surveying the tents, he mused that it was not as easy as he thought, and not totally without risk. For as Speaker, who had assumed the powers of the White Throne, he had also assumed its downsides. It was in his charge to lead the Empire's armies, at times, into war. And in that capacity he was not as far from danger as he had hoped. Forward Camp itself, diminished in size due to casualties, was on the edge of what was called the Ugar Coast. There were reports every day of raiding parties, of emboldened citizens of Eioli driving out Imperials and Imperial sympathizers wherever they went. Here, on the border, Lornodoris was not completely protected.

And morale had plummeted.

Lornodoris had only begun to see the effects of the war, but they had begun to frighten him.

He had seen legionaries with amputated arms and legs. He had seen, largely for the first time, the effects of the Empire's conquests. And in the Council House such matters of war, such matters of life and death, were relegated to debate and the passage of laws; they were never real, or at least they had not been.

A man was sitting at the entrance of a tent, clutching his knees and mumbling to himself. He seemed to have bloated, though there were no missing limbs, no outward sign of injury.

But among those veterans of the first Siege of Eioli, those who had not been sentenced to die for cowardice, there seemed a different kind of wound… a wound of the mind.

Those who shook and babbled, who had to be restrained, were considered to have "the divine disease." They were said to be touched by the gods.

But this was entirely different. The legionaries afflicted by this condition, the survivors of the first Siege of Eioli, were not touched by the gods at all. For in their mad eyes Lornodoris could see nightmares; and their shaking never stopped. Silently they writhed, without cease, and on some of their bodies there were ghastly, bright red sores. They could not tell the legates what happened during the siege; they could only sit there, chatter and babble.

As he looked upon the veteran, who had survived the siege, Lornodoris recalled the conversations that he had had with Councilor Valerius. Valerius had claimed the Ugars worshipped strange gods, and implied that somehow powers had been summoned.

It was impossible, Lornodoris knew. But when he saw the horror of Forward Camp, when he saw the survivors of the first siege, he began to wonder. What could have caused such strange injuries? What natural forces, what elements of the physical world, could make a man sit there and babble, to look on in a far-eyed stare of fear?

But Eioli would be brought to heel soon enough.

Still the fear lingered, the worry that there was something

more than appeared.

The legions were on the move; the Second and Third Peregothian, the Sixth Anthanian Legions were on their way. The Fourth Kerundian Legion was already in enemy territory, preparing siege instruments.

And Agatho Lornodoris had been appointed grand legate over them all. It was his task to crush Eioli, to strategize, to prepare a way where there had not been a way before. He had tried to research why the Fourth Peregothian had turned and fled, at a time when victory was at hand. But all he had heard was supernatural nonsense: a driving fear, a horrid spirit swirling through the ranks.

The Fourth Peregothian had been thought to be the best; formed in the crucible of the peninsula's conquest, it was the only legion whose record had been spotless, only victories registered and never defeats.

The Sixth Anthanian Legion, newly formed, was filled with green recruits.

And as Lornodoris surveyed Forward Camp, so empty, so full of sickness and disease, he began to worry all over again. He wondered—though he would admit it to no one—whether he was up to the task, whether the position of Grand Legate was a fit for him.

Eioli awaited. And as soon as the legions arrived, they would move.

Chapter Forty-Six

Publius Allius Corvus, Legionary

A full legionary, Publius was.

He had achieved the goal of his childhood, the goal of his youth. He'd now be paid a handsome salary. He'd see the world. He would risk his life, yes, but that was part of the job.

The Sixth Anthanian Legion, newly assembled, was beginning to gather about fifty miles east of the Ugar Coast.

There was a mix of green recruits and veterans. Publius' centurion was a longtime veteran named Nichus.

The grass was yellow, desiccated. Hills stretched into the interminable distance. Far away there was the green outline of woodland. It was amazing how close they were to a region of rich soil and well-watered fields. Here, fifty miles out, was a desolation, a wilderness.

Lucius and he had been separated; Lucius had been assigned to the Third Peregothian. He had been lucky, for it was filled with veterans, experienced troops who had seen the ravages of war and the desperation of it.

One thousand men were here out of three thousand, but the Sixth Anthanian Legion would be assembled within days.

Their grand legate was a man named Agatho Lornodoris. Publius knew nothing about him.

Publius by himself, headed out to the outskirts of camp. He had his sword with him. He was getting used to the weight of his armor and shield, trying to remember what he had been taught about his sword: thrust, slash, thrust. In the right situations, the legion was an unstoppable, immovable force, invincible to most other armies. The barbarians of Eioli wouldn't stand a chance.

"Hey! You!" A voice was calling after him, and in the

surprise of the moment he thought it was Julia.

But he turned, and no, it was a legionary, a young man, not a woman.

He was not wearing his helmet, but his armor was shimmering in the sun. Over his breastplate he had the standard red-gold tabard.

His hair was auburn, his face freckled. His eyes were brown.

"Are you from Victory Camp?"

"No," Publius answered. "Blue Eagle."

There was a pause; the young man looked surprised.

"Well, I'm Rufus," he said. "I thought I recognized you. I guess I was wrong."

Rufus walked over, drew closer. Buckled to his belt was the standard-issue Imperial sword that every legionary was given.

Rufus had to be younger than Publius by a few years. He could tell it by the tone in his voice, the naivety of his words. Perhaps, Rufus didn't know what he was getting himself into. Perhaps, Publius didn't either.

"Are you ready?" Publius said. "Are you ready to lay siege to Eioli?"

"Did you hear?" Rufus said. "They've declared war on every city of the coast. We won't get out of here for months, at best. A new war! I bet people back in the city love the idea."

Publius could tell by Rufus' accent he hailed from the city. But he did not speak with the aloof dialect of an August. He was probably common like Publius, a citizen with rights, who could vote and serve in the legions, but not a noble.

In truth, Publius wanted to be alone. But it seemed this Rufus had latched on to him.

"I think Eioli will be a tough problem!" Rufus said. "Did you hear the Fourth Peregothian broke on them? The Fourth Peregothian! The Fourth Peregothian!

"They had the Ugars where they wanted them, and then,

one night, they all fled in different directions. They retired the entire legion. A sad end for it, I'd say."

The Fourth Peregothian was indeed the stuff of legend, having never suffered a defeat in its more than a century of service. But Rufus' words troubled Publius. They were on the verge of a victory, and then the veteran soldiers, who had seen the horrors and ravages of war, broke like a bunch of yellow cowards?

"They fled?" Publius said. He had assumed they had been defeated by force. But he had been wrong.

"Yes, it's the strangest thing," Rufus said. "They had just about broken down the gate. Eioli looked like it was about to surrender. And then… then night fell. Something happened. They all ran away. And some are sick, truly sick. I don't like the look of them…"

Rufus' words were puzzling, puzzling and frightening. Publius wondered what could change so suddenly, what veterans of the Empire's most famous legion could have seen that had made them turn and run.

"Well, I'm Publius," he said. "I guess we'll be fighting the Ugars together."

"Yes," Rufus said, "yes we will, brother."

Brothers-in-arms was a quaint term, but Publius would live with it for now. He had greater concerns, like the land just beyond the camp, a strange land that defied description, and a city that had caused veteran soldiers to break like cowards.

Chapter Forty-Seven

Publius Allius Corvus, Legionary

The campfire was burning and Publius, for better or for worse, was sitting next to Rufus. They and their fellow legionaries, a mix of green recruits and veterans, had gathered around the flame. Most all of them were young, some from the city, some from the rural districts. All of them were Imperial citizens. All of them were going to Eioli.

On a skewer Publius was roasting a cut of lamb. Wine was flowing freely, but he had not partaken.

The night was deep and the crickets were chirping with an intoxicating rhythm.

"Who is ready?" some drunk legionary said. "Who is ready? We will conquer Eioli… and then help ourselves to the Ugar women."

Publius winced.

"Ah, no," said another legionary. "Ugar women… they will do in a pinch. But I like women who are less hairy than me."

There was scattered laughter, but Publius stood up and left in disgust. The lamb was hardly cooked and there was just a sear on its outside edge. But better to eat it raw than to listen to such talk.

Yet there was commotion up ahead; in the light of the campfires, Publius could see a black coach arriving, the kind that accompanied announcements of death.

One of the centurions was there talking to a dark hooded man. On the outside of the coach, the gold eagle insignia of the Empire was emblazoned. It was official business, and the hooded man was carrying a letter.

The centurion shouted, "Publius Corvus!" and in an instant his stomach clenched. He did not want to hear the news, if there

was any bad news. He was about to embark on the siege of Eioli;
he could not do it with the burden of grief.

But the centurion was a centurion, ranking high above
Publius.

Publius started at a walk, then began to hurry toward him.

"Publius," the centurion said. "There is bad news."

The hooded man's face was pallid; he had a somber
expression on your face.

"Publius Corvus," the hooded man started. "Your father
Caius has died."

In an instant Publius' heart sank; the world seemed to
collapse all around him, and he himself dragged into a dark abyss.
"No… it can't be…"

"I am afraid it is so," the hooded man said. "And the
funeral rites are soon. You are being recalled for a temporary leave
from the Sixth Anthanian Legion. You will return when you have
finished your familial duty."

His father… his father… it couldn't be.

"So I will not fight?" Publius said. Tears were forming in
his eyes, though he did not want to show emotion.

"We would not want to upset your father's spirit," the
hooded man said. "Collect your belongings, legionary, and come
with me."

~

It was the moment his world shattered, a moment he would
forever remember. Unwound and undone, trying not to weep, he
staggered into the coach, knowing his father was in a better place
but he in a much worse one.

Chapter Forty-Eight

Agatho Lornodoris, Speaker of the Council, Grand Legate

The morning sun was shining over Forward Camp. The sky was blue and there was not a single cloud drifting through the firmament. It was the day Agatho had selected to invade.

In terms of weather, he could not have hoped for a better day. Before him the legions were massing, twenty thousand soldiers, young men, the nation's finest. There was no trace of wind to halt their arrows; the calculations of the siege engineers—of whom the Imperials had an impossible advantage—would be spot on.

With the legions were auxiliaries, troops of northern barbarians and lines of Kheroan cavalry, and several battalions of archers from the Eastern Kingdoms.

All was well. His plans had all been realized; everything was in its place. So why, then, was his heart fluttering in his chest? Why did his hands feel clammy, so clammy he kept looking at them, fearing that others would see? Why did he have a splitting headache, and this irrational, obsessive thought that he was growing horns?

Fools like Councilor Valerius would say it had a supernatural explanation. But Lornodoris was first and foremost a rationalist, and the prior night he had instructed the apothecary to give him something for the headaches.

But the medicine, a powder he had mixed in with last night's wine, had not worked in the slightest. In fact, when he had woken up this morning, the headaches had become unbearable, like knives piercing into his skull. And the delusions had gotten worse. When he first woke up, he had looked in the mirror, sure something was growing underneath his skin. He had scratched and scratched until he bled. He had masked the cuts with pigment, but every time he looked at a tribune or an Imperial agent he was sure he had done a poor job, that there were open wounds on his forehead for all to see.

And battle… battle awaited.

The Ugar armies outnumbered them in theory, but the Imperial troops so outclassed them the odds were a million to one of victory.

That was what he told himself. The primitive Ugars would likely surrender as soon as they saw the legions marching toward them, the legions with their red-gold standards, the gleaming metal of their breastplates, the crimson of their horsehair crests.

A tribune was walking toward him from the edge of camp.

"Signor Legate," he said and gave a slight bow.

The term of honor had once tickled his ego, but now it frightened him; and underneath the surface he had begun to admit to himself he wasn't fit for it, he wasn't fit for it at all.

"The troops await your command," the tribune continued. "At your orders, we will march."

"March, then," Lornodoris said. "To Eioli we go."

Chapter Forty-Nine

Quintus Marcus Rufus, Legionary

Rufus did not understand why he was shaking, why, last night, he had dreamed of a deep darkness, but two lights like eyes were piercing it. He had woken up exhausted, covered in goose prickles, with hardly a breath in his lungs.

And now they were marching, yes, they were marching, into the daylight, into the bright light of the sun. Birds were singing and the air was pleasantly warm. But they were venturing away from the Empire; they were venturing into a land of dark rich silt, and unfathomable nightmare.

Chapter Fifty

Publius Allius Corvus, Legionary

Turning and twisting, writhing in the back of the coach, Publius spent the third night since his departure overcome by dreams.

He dreamed first of the dark temple and the mountain road, but then, then his dreams turned to the tomb where his father was laying.

A creature was there, on all fours, helping itself to his father's bones, chewing on sinew and cartilage.

But no, it was not a creature; it was a person.

It turned, clutching a chewed off hand in its mouth, and he saw it was a woman there, a woman on all fours as if she was a beast.

Julia… it was Julia, though her face was dark and her eyes hollow. It was Julia there… it was Julia in his father's tomb.

Epilude

The people of Imperial City were confident, yes, they were confident on that bright and warm autumn morning.

The end has not come, they said. No, it has not come.

The skies were red once… and now they were blue.

Glossary

Anthania: A large peninsula, with the Middle Sea on its eastern edge and the ocean on its west. It is named after Anthans the Conqueror.

Anthans: A famed Imperial legate who conquered much of what is now called the Anthania Peninsula.

Augusts: The higher of the two tiers of Imperial nobility, with those under them being called knights. They are the descendants of the original founders of the Empire.

Barbarian: A derogative term for a person who is neither Imperial nor from the Eastern Kingdoms.

Canal District: A ward of Imperial city, located adjacent to the harbor.

Council House, the: A tower-like structure that dominates the Imperial City skyline, its construction was begun not long after the initial conquest of the Anthanian peninsula.

Century: The smallest division of the Imperial army, composed of about one-hundred to two-hundred men, under the command of an official called a centurion.

Eastern Kingdoms, the: A term for the rich, ancient lands of Eloesus on the opposite shore, far east across the Middle Sea.

Eioli: Considered the queen city of Ugarit, it is the region's richest and most storied city. It has dominated Ugarit for centuries.

Emperor: The leader of the empire, taking on some of the roles of a king, but heavily checked by the power of the Imperial Council.

Flamens: A secretive group of sorcerers believed to have powers of invisibility and far-sight.

Grand Legate: The commander appointed to control several legions.

Goldenhorn Mountains: Large snowcapped mountains abutting the northwestern edge of the Anthanian Peninsula. They are filled with iron mines and silver mines.

Imperial City: The largest city of the Empire, considered its heart. Its legal name is Anthans, named after the conqueror of the peninsula.

Imperial Council: A semi-democratic branch of the Imperial government, formed by thirty men voted for by the free citizens of Imperial City's thirty wards.

Imperial Guard: A group of about a hundred veterans of the legions, considered an elite fighting force. They are tasked with guarding the emperor.

Laconus Lornodoris: The founder of a branch of the Lornodoris family, a famed councilor and statesman who fought in the conquest of Anthania. Like the other Lornodorises, they arise from old Peregothian stock, from the time of the founding of the city.

Legate: The commander of a legion.

Legion: The largest division of the Imperial armies, composed of around five thousand men.

Legis: An expert on the procedures of the Imperial Council. He can only be overruled in certain circumstances, and even then on a two-thirds or sometimes unanimous vote.

Middle Sea, the: An immense sea in the center of the world. The Empire lies on its westernmost edge.

Paradise Gardens: A resort town for the rich in the foothills of the Goldenhorn Mountains. Members of the Imperial Council often retreat there at the height of summer.

Kheroe: A city-state directly south of the Anthanian peninsula, across the sea. It is known for its strange customs and its ancient wealth. They are one of the oldest of the Empire's allies.

Knight: The lower of two tiers of the Imperial nobility.

Traditionally they were seen as the Empire's soldiers, but that distinction has faded. Now, many of the Knightly class have no connections to the military.

Seladora: The goddess of woodlands, the gentle side of nature, and nymphs.

Suburro: A poor ward of Imperial City, located just outside Imperial Square.

Ugar: A native of the land of Ugarit.

Ugarit: A land on the Anthanian peninsula's west-central coast, dominated by the three cities of Eioli, Tikal and Hoda. They are noted for their customs that are very different from the other people groups of the peninsula.

Unification. the: Considered one of the founding events of the Empire, the Unification occurred when the Formusus and Tenebarius tribes united under one king, establishing a kingdom on the island of Peregoth. A series of seven kings, called by some the Sea Kings, ruled until they were overthrown and a semi-democratic system was formed.

Urban Cohorts: The only legion that is allowed to reside in Imperial City, they are under the direct command of the Imperial Guard and the emperor. In addition to protecting the city, they act as a kind of police force, keeping the peace and upholding the law.

About the Author

Cursed at birth with a wild imagination, Andrew Cooper spent his youth dreaming of worlds more exciting than Earth.

He is a graduate of the Odyssey Writing Workshop. His stories have appeared in Morpheus Tales, Fear and Trembling, Residential Aliens and Mindflights, among others.

Contact the Author

Visit **www.aj-cooper.com** to sign up for the newsletter and stay up-to-date on new releases.

Find him on Facebook at:

www.facebook.com/AJCooperauthor